# Praise for Joely Skye's
## *Monster, Zombie, & Minder*

"Josh is an alpha male without being a jerk: he's noble, capable and action-oriented, but also generous, kind and tender. (You know, the kind of hero I wish I could find in a straight romance.)...As MONSTER reached its cliffhanger, the author gave a few peeks into the dark sides of Minder culture. I took it as a promise that the two future installments will explore those shadows further. I look forward to the trip."

*~ Joyce Ellen Armond, Speculative Romance Online*

"...a beautiful story..."

*~ Shannon, Joyfully Reviewed*

Rating: 4 Stars Heat level: H "...Ms. Skye has created an emotionally engaging, saddening, and somehow loving story...Their lovemaking is tender, sensual, and sizzling at the same time, with just a hint of the love that may come in the future. Unfortunately, Kir's ability as a Minder leaves Josh with a taste of distrust and leaves the reader wondering what may happen next. With two more installments coming in the future, I can hardly wait to see how their relationship develops into more."

*~ Caye Kimberley, Just Erotic Romance Reviews*

Rating: 4/5 Stars Heat level: H "...a hauntingly beautiful tale...I felt like I was intruding on a love story and the emotions in their sexual encounter, while not scorching, were wonderful...A breathtaking story, the series will continue with the roles being reversed, and I for one, cannot wait."

~ *Stacey Landers, Just Erotic Romance Reviews*

4 1/2 Stars! "Zombie is a really enjoyable and intriguing book; the fast pace and good understanding of character will keep every reader racing along toward the conclusion...Joely Skye is a writer I will definitely keep on my watch-for list."

~ *Annie, Ecataromance Sensual*

"Zombie is one of those books that grabbed my attention immediately, I liked both characters and they seem to grow emotionally as the story moves on...Zombie is not your normal formula romance, but it's a fantastic story, and I will defiantly be on the look out for the next one in this intriguing series."

~ *Julia, The Romance Studio*

"The Minders series reads like a serial and is just as addictive...Haunting and unforgettable, ZOMBIE will leave you clamoring for more of this series."

~ *Isabelle Spencer, RRT Erotic*

"...the conflict is just incredible. I don't want to reveal any spoilers, but holy cow, folks. Skye works the conflict of psychics vs. normals so well, and puts into peril this fascinating Josh-Kir relationship so completely, that she could write the ending in Morse Code and I'd read it."

~ *JE Armond, Speculative Romance*

"Zombie is the second book in the Minder series and even more powerful than the first...Ms. Skye has penned another deeply emotional and sexy tale for her captivating men. Readers will find themselves at the edge of their seats trying to predict the outcome, but the startling twist in the end is anything but predictable."

*~ Water Nymph, Literary Nymphs Reviews*


"Ms. Skye has continued the Minders series with another very creative and well written book. The control that the agency has over Josh is so realistic that it is frightening."

*~ Teresa, Fallen Angel Reviews*


"If you love sexy, twisted tales and a conspiracy theory or two, do not miss this superbly intense series."

*~ Isabelle Spencer, RRTErotic*


5 Nymphs! "Ms. Skye's scorching love scenes are as hot as they are sweet, and the sizzling romance between Josh and Kir will touch your heart. Readers will enthusiastically devour the pages until the very end, an ending that may leave you sniffling and will certainly leave you smiling."

*~ Literary Nymphs Reviews*


5 Lips! "Joely Skye's excellent Minders trilogy continues with Minder, the third volume. Readers once again will thrill to the rapid plot pace and to the ups and downs of the characters. Minder is a sort of espionage wrapped in suspense wrapped in mental and physical violence wrapped in character angst wrapped in gay romance and intimacy story."

*~ Frost, Two Lips Reviews*

# Beautiful Monster

*Joely Skye*

A SAMHAIN PUBLISHING, LTD. publication.

Samhain Publishing, Ltd.
512 Forest Lake Drive
Warner Robins, GA 31093
www.samhainpublishing.com

Beautiful Monster
Copyright © 2007 by Joely Skye
Print ISBN: 1-59998-568-3

Monster Digital ISBN: 1-59998-130-0
Zombie Digital ISBN: 1-59998-174-2
Minder Digital ISBN: 1-59998-333-8

Editing by Sasha Knight
Cover by Vanessa Hawthorne

First Monster, Ltd. electronic publication: July 2006
First Zombie, Ltd. electronic publication: November 2006
First Minder, Ltd. electronic publication: February 2007
First Samhain Publishing, Ltd. print publication: August 2007

# Contents

# Monster

# Dedication

For my husband.

# Chapter One

Joshua Mackay was hunting a monster by bicycle. In the park. On a Sunday afternoon.

And he'd lost sight of his quarry. Sweat soaked his clothes as he pumped his legs, taking the path's curves as quickly as possible. Which wasn't all that fast given that the family activity brigade was out in full force. He swiped a hand over his face and wished it wasn't ninety-degree weather. Salt stung his eyes and he squinted, looking ahead. Surely the monster hadn't escaped.

He'd been careful, perhaps so careful he hadn't actually poked a hole in the back wheel of the monster's bike. Surreptitious was all well and good, but not when it meant failure. He had thought to find Kiran Brunner with a flat tire by now.

Perhaps the monster was even more talented than Josh had been led to believe. Kir made men forget him, or bent them to his will. Most spectacularly, he had once convinced a man to shoot himself in the head. Fortunately, Josh carried a bicycle pump, not a gun. He might be compelled to brain himself with a pump but he didn't think it would be fatal.

He biked here every day in the summer. The monster that was, not Josh who preferred air-conditioning over smoggy heat. Baking in the sun was hell and even if evil belonged there, Josh didn't. Besides, Josh didn't believe in evil so much as capability and Kir, as his files named him, was capable of murder.

Not that you could tell by the photos and videos Josh had studied over the past month. There the boy's expression was mostly grim, occasionally sullen. Wide-spaced eyes, a mobile mouth and defined cheekbones made Kir's dark gaze profoundly disturbing. And beautiful, in a wild way.

Kir had become his obsession since Josh had taken this job. His contact wanted Kir alive. To study. To track down the other dangerous Minders who could invade and destroy people's minds. So Josh prepared to meet this beautiful monster on a warm, green summer day.

Speak of the devil. There he was, walking his crippled bike down the asphalt path.

Josh slowed while adrenaline spilled out of his nerves and fed his blood. The next few minutes were critical. As planned, his brakes squeaked in warning. He didn't want to startle Kir, who was a jumpy kind of guy. Went with the psi territory and, no doubt, with being on the agency's most-wanted list. A potent combination.

As Josh approached, Kir jerked to a stop and whipped his head around. Hands clenched the bike's handlebars while his entire body stiffened. *Casual*, Josh warned himself. He stood, straddling his bike, leaving enough distance not to crowd the jittery boy.

Josh wiped his face again, giving the monster time to get used to his presence. He hadn't planned to be sweating like a pig when he finally talked to Kir, but it couldn't be helped.

"Flat?" Josh glanced at Kir's back wheel.

"Yeah." Kir's tone implied, *what of it?*

"I've got a repair kit."

Kir didn't respond, just watched Josh warily.

Josh shrugged. "If you want to borrow it. Otherwise I'll be on my way." He sat back on his seat and lifted one foot to the pedal.

Kir stared, unblinking, but just before Josh was about to push off, Kir said, "Okay." The one word came out a little breathlessly. "Thanks," he added with a halfhearted grin. The boy wasn't used to smiling and the awkward effort surprised Josh.

"Sure." Josh walked his bike off the path.

"Where's the kit?" Kir asked. Josh had the impression he was trying not to sound suspicious.

"Here." Josh unzipped the pouch under his bicycle seat. There he carried the repair kit, a pump and a garage-door opener—access to the safe house. Safe for him. Not so safe for Kir.

Josh handed over the cheap kit and Kir took it with a jerk.

"Thanks," he mumbled.

"You can keep it. Do you have your own pump?" Josh knew he didn't.

"No. But if you're in a hurry..."

Josh leaned against a tree. "I'm not." He kept his smile on low beam. "I can wait. You can use mine."

Kir held his gaze for a moment, going wide-eyed.

*Oh, baby, don't tell me you're easy.* This *was the monster the agency had hunted for over a year?*

"Thanks," Kir repeated. A man of few words. A *monster* of few words, Josh reminded himself. It was all well and good to get into his role here but he shouldn't forget Kir was a twenty-two-year-old psychotic Minder.

Kir crouched down and went to work while Josh eyed him. Just as well the boy wore loose clothing. Josh didn't need the distraction right now. Dark eyes and faux naiveté were bad enough. Not that Josh pursued youth or inexperience but he had an unrewarding protective streak that was easily aroused.

Rather than openly admire the boy's body, he watched the families walk, bike and skate past on the all-purpose asphalt path. Kir came here every day and Josh had chosen to catch him on Sunday when the crowd could explain his own presence and make him less of a perceived threat.

A couple of minutes later Kir rose with a sheepish expression. "I never get flats. I don't know what happened today."

"Glass, maybe."

He frowned. "I don't think so. I didn't see any."

"Would you like to use the pump?" Josh brandished his.

"Thanks."

"You sure are polite. That's the fourth time you've thanked me."

Kir ducked his head endearingly and Josh wondered if he were being played. Fine, let the boy think he was in control and Josh was charmed by his artless act. Josh passed the pump and made finger contact.

Shivering, Kir pulled away. Psis often didn't like to be touched, but the boy's expression conveyed surprise, not recoil. He crouched down quickly, though not before Josh observed a flush.

*This is like taking candy from a baby.* "I hardly ever use this park, though I live nearby."

Kir glanced at him. "I come here all the time. When it's cooler, I run."

"I'm not surprised. You have runner's legs."

Instead of acknowledging the compliment, Kir concentrated on attaching the pump to the tire.

"Actually, I'm glad I stopped," continued Josh. "The sun is getting to me. I'm heading home for a drink soon."

Kir worked the pump furiously and Josh waited, giving the boy time to absorb what was happening. When he was done, Kir rose and wiped his face on the sleeve of his T-shirt.

"I hope you have lots of water," said Josh.

"Uh, some." Kir stood on the balls of his feet, ready to spring. Under normal circumstances, Josh would never move on someone so skittish.

"Come back to my place and hydrate yourself." Josh kept his words light.

Kir stared, as if he were a deer caught in headlights, and Josh was annoyed that a part of him felt bad. Either the monster was a very good actor, or he really couldn't decide whether or not to accept the invitation.

"Can I have my pump?" Josh held out his hand.

"Oh. Yeah."

This time Josh didn't force the finger contact. He just took the pump and attached it to his bike. Kir watched as Josh slung a leg over the bicycle's bar. "Coming?" he asked, as if it were no big deal.

Kir blinked. "Okay."

"Follow me." Josh set off and didn't look back.

As he sped up, he wondered if he'd played it too cool. For a real hookup, he would have pushed harder to make Kir know he was wanted. But in this situation, the less Josh appeared to care, the better. The boy had good reason to be suspicious. The agency had been hunting him for a year now and he'd had some close calls. The failures had inspired the agency to use an outsider to lure the monster back to his cage. A gay outsider who might connect to the boy who occasionally had anonymous sex with men.

Josh braked at the stop sign and only then glanced back to see Kir hot on his trail. Good.

"Just down the road." Josh left the bike path and entered suburbia. There they rode side by side. Kir gazed with open admiration at the upscale houses they passed, which amused Josh, or would have if he wasn't wound so tight. The endgame was in sight.

Josh led Kir to the two-story, five-bedroom house he'd become acquainted with this past week.

"Wow. Is this yours?" Kir was impressed.

"Yup," Josh lied. "Accountants know how to pay their bills." He turned away from the boy's admiration and thumbed the garage-door opener. The white double door folded up into the garage's ceiling.

"Come on in," said Josh.

Kir hung back as Josh wheeled his bike in beside the black SUV taking up half of the garage.

"I'm ready for air conditioning. You?"

"Okay." Kir took a deep breath and followed Josh, parking his bike. They entered the house and, once the door shut behind them, Josh breathed a little more easily. The boy didn't know it, but he was locked in.

"Water? Juice? Something stronger?" Josh asked as he walked to the kitchen. Kir trailed behind him.

"Water, please."

Josh turned to see Kir wince, as if he thought he sounded stupid. Somehow, Josh hadn't expected the boy to be naive.

Kir gave a sharp shake of the head. "Sorry, I'm just not used to..."

"Getting picked up during the day?" Josh let his smile widen. Kir jerked his shoulders in an attempt to shrug. While he fidgeted, Josh pulled down two glasses from the cupboard and filled them with water.

"There's a first time for everything." Josh didn't touch Kir's fingers as he handed him the glass. It was too close to the end. This cat and mouse game left him with a bad taste in his mouth. Monster or not, Kir was too easily played. The files had led Josh to expect some sophistication, especially about sex.

Kir gulped down the entire glass at once. *Too fast.* Josh resisted the impulse to shake his head at Kir. God, with a little show of interest, of *concern*, anyone could have brought this boy in.

"Thanks." Kir swiped his mouth.

"I think you should stop thanking me," Josh said gently.

Kir's face softened, as if he thought Josh was about to seduce him. When Josh didn't do anything, Kir's expression clouded. He pointed to Josh's full glass of water. "I thought you were thirsty."

"I am." Josh drank—the drug had been in Kir's glass, not in the water. The boy's frown remained. Josh wondered, in an idle, theoretical way, if Kir would realize Josh had duped him and exact revenge before passing out. The agency had stressed how easily Kir could damage Josh's mind. Maybe the drug wasn't strong enough for the boy.

The boy. Josh felt like a shit. Perhaps Kir had manipulated him into guilt without his realizing it. This was Kir's talent, using words to convince people they were acting on their own cognizance.

But Josh was unharmed while Kir staggered and reached for the table. Today Josh had done damage, not Kir.

"You okay?" Josh made no move to help.

"Yes." Kir's confusion belied his word. He stared intently at the table's edge, trying to pull himself together. "I..." Realization dawned though Horton, Josh's contact, had sworn the drug wouldn't allow it. "Oh." Kir blinked up at Josh. "You?" Disappointment gave way to something else—determination. Kir's gaze intensified, even as his body trembled against the drug, and Josh couldn't look away.

"Don't let them hurt me." Kir's face drained of color and he fell forward.

Josh moved quickly. The least he could do was break the boy's fall. Bending his knees, he caught Kir and scooped him up. He wasn't light for his height, but he wasn't tall either, and Josh was strong.

The boy smelled good, young, fresh. *What a waste.* Kir should be out with friends on the weekend, not trying—and failing—to escape the agency. Josh carried him to the couch. Laid him down. In his forced sleep the boy looked incredibly innocent—long eyelashes, smooth face with just a hint of the day's stubble.

But Josh knew about innocence. It wasn't always pure. He dialed his contact. "He's here," he said. "He's out."

# Chapter Two

Five minutes later, the man Josh knew as Thompson walked through the front door with a duffel bag in one hand. Thompson was the muscle—big, strong and practical, with an incongruously kind face. Josh neither liked nor trusted him.

"It's done," said Josh, for lack of anything better to say.

Thompson grunted. "We haven't much time. Did he drink the whole dose?"

"Yes." Josh pointed to the couch.

Thompson strode over, grinned down at Kir and shook his head. "Sleeping like a baby. Well, not for long, eh?"

Josh didn't like the comment, then wondered why he cared. His work here was done.

Thompson pulled an envelope out of his bag and threw it on the coffee table. "That's for you. Get out."

"Where's Snow?" Josh had a bad feeling about leaving Kir with Thompson. Snow was Kir's handler. Or had been, in the days when Kir was manageable. Surely that meant Snow would protect Kir to some extent.

Thompson walked back to Josh and gazed down at him, as if to assess how serious he was. Or perhaps to intimidate. "I told them you were soft. They said it didn't matter."

"I just don't want him hurt."

Thompson laughed. "Where'd you get that idea from? Kir?"

Josh frowned. He didn't think so.

Thompson jabbed his thumb backwards. "He'll want to hurt you. You just betrayed him, remember?" When Josh didn't react, Thompson lost interest in the conversation. "I don't have time for this." He returned to Kir's side and got to work.

He taped Kir's mouth shut, pulled a black hood over his head and threw the boy over his shoulder like a sack of potatoes. Thompson walked down the hall to the soundproof room that protected people from Kir's poisonous words.

Josh's heart beat too fast and it wasn't the rush of a job well done. Thompson's heavy, slow tread, Kir's arms hanging down, the black hood bobbing against Thompson's back—it all disturbed him, though he'd known restraint was absolutely necessary.

For God's sakes, Kir was psi—a Minder—who needed to be brought under control. Still, pressure built in Josh's chest and he blew out air, as if that would relieve his distress.

Horton wanted Josh out as quickly as possible; had some concerns about contamination by the mutant. But Josh could check on Kir at a distance, to make sure he was okay. Josh walked into the den and flipped on the screen that showed the soundproof room.

Kir's body, naked and slack, hung over some kind of contraption.

"Fuck!" he swore at the screen. What, exactly, had he just accomplished? The agency had appeared completely neutral on the subject of Kir's sexuality and his contact had assured Josh he wasn't about to become involved in some kind of gay witch hunt. Psi was the overwhelming issue. Dangerous. Murderous.

Josh stared at the unconscious nude body. He swung away from the screen and marched down the hall, shoving open the

20

door so it slammed against the wall. "What the fuck are you doing?" he demanded of Thompson.

Closer now, he could see Kir's feet were shackled and he stood spread-eagled, or would have if he were conscious. As it was, he half lay over a vaulting horse similar to one Josh had used in elementary school many years ago.

Thompson barely glanced at Josh as he handcuffed Kir's wrists to poles on either side of the vault.

"Getting ready to spank him?" Josh asked harshly.

"Could be," mused Thompson as he finished the job. Kir's hands were raised above his head. This was not a position of comfort. "There, all done, and before the patient awakes, which is critical..." Thompson turned, "Do yourself a favor and get out of here before you hurt yourself."

Josh swallowed. "I did not bring him in to be stripped and shackled."

"We do what is necessary." Thompson spoke matter-of-factly. "Kir needs to be kept away from his magic. Otherwise he might convince me to shoot myself in the head, or something."

"And wouldn't that be a shame," Josh ground out. "Look, asshole, this isn't how you treat prisoners, and I don't give a fuck what they can do."

Thompson's mouth twisted into a cynical smile. "Yeah? Interesting."

Kir groaned through the tape and hood.

Thompson smiled. "Heh, just in time. Sleeping beauty is about to awake."

The boy stiffened.

"You worked fast on this one, Kir," said Thompson cheerfully. "Congratulations. I think you've just signed his death warrant."

"What are you talking about?" Josh loathed Thompson's manner.

Thompson turned away, placing a hand on Kir's naked shoulder. Kir twitched it off as best he could but Thompson pressed down until Kir came alive. His entire body bucked while he screamed. Having the scream muffled, if not strangled, by the tape around his mouth, made the noise that much worse.

"That's enough." But Thompson ignored Josh and Kir continued to struggle.

"There, there." Thompson touched Kir's arm, making the boy wilder.

Josh stepped closer. "Back off," he warned Thompson.

Thompson raised his eyebrows. "Or?" He went to touch Kir again and Josh landed a kick on the man's solar plexus, hard enough to wind without doing damage. Thompson ended up on his ass.

"You're an idiot." He rubbed his stomach. His words were soft, but his tone furious. A muscle jumped in his jaw as he reached for the sidearm Josh knew Thompson carried. Before he could cock the gun, Josh kicked it out of his hand and it flew across the room.

"This is torture. It's illegal. I do not hand over my targets so people can *play* with them."

Thompson shook his head. "The only damage Kir has so far sustained was from the drug you gave him. He needs to be restrained for everyone's safety. I was testing those restraints."

"Testing." Josh's sarcasm was heavy, overwrought.

"He'd kill you in a blink of an eye."

"I expect a certain standard of behavior, not this bullshit."

Thompson rolled his eyes. "You're not even a government agent. You're freelance and this is the crap we get."

"You mean, crap like integrity? That's just too fucking bad for you." Josh had to control his rage or he'd start shaking. "I'm going to wait here until Snow arrives."

"Snow, huh?" Thompson's eyelids drooped in something akin to disgust. Then he glanced over at Kir. "Look, our little tête-à-tête is calming you down, eh Kir?"

Kir didn't move.

Thompson kept talking in his odd, cheerful way, as if Josh's actions were not to be taken seriously. "Our mutual friend here—who set you up, Kir, in case you hadn't figured that out—is having second thoughts. Quick work on your part, I have to say."

In the silence that followed, Josh listened to Kir breathe noisily, as if he couldn't get enough air. "He's suffocating."

"Don't worry. He's just having a panic attack. He might pass out, but he never gets asphyxiated. I know how to look after him."

"For God's sakes," Josh muttered.

"You want to take that tape off his mouth?"

"No." He wasn't stupid, he just expected professional behavior. After this debacle he was going to avoid any and all work with Horton and the agency.

"Go ahead," said Thompson as if Josh hadn't spoken. "Kir will be anxious to thank you."

Josh walked over to where he'd kicked the gun, picked it up and pointed it at Thompson. "Let's leave Kir alone for a few moments. That way you can't torment him."

Thompson laughed. "Don't tell me you're in love with him, too."

"I am not 'in love' with him."

"I don't see it myself, but I like women."

"How nice for you." Josh waved him towards the door but Thompson stepped deeper into the room. Angry enough to shoot a limb, Josh removed the safety and faced Thompson full on. "Wrong way."

"Yeah."

"You think I won't shoot?"

Kir made a strangled noise while Thompson stared straight at Josh. "I think you won't shoot," he said quietly. Thompson's gaze shifted to the right.

Josh felt air move just before something hammered down on the back of his head. Pain smashed through his vision and he dropped the gun. Stupid, he thought as he fell without quite losing consciousness. He'd known Thompson didn't work alone.

His vision grayed out, then in, then out. He was vaguely aware of another person in the room, as well as a strange, low noise. It took a moment to realize he was groaning. Agony echoed through his head and he couldn't think.

"What the hell is going on?" said the new voice.

"He's trying to save Kir." Thompson this time.

"Ah. Kir is nothing, if not resourceful."

As Josh's pain softened, he realized someone was groping him, emptying pockets, finding two knives and his cell phone.

"He had your gun, Thom."

"Yeah." Thompson sounded rather grumpy.

A boot tip prodded Josh's chest. With some effort, Josh opened his eyes. A man with blond, shaggy hair looked down. Snow. Kir's handler. Josh had thought the man's arrival would improve the situation.

"Hello. Kir, darling, did you fall for a brunette with freckles? How quaint."

Josh turned over and tried to rise, but fell on his face.

"Isn't that cute? He's trying to get up." Snow's tone changed as he addressed Thompson again. "You could have avoided this mess by escorting him off the premises."

"I didn't have time and he wouldn't leave. Kept yammering on about professional standards."

Snow sighed. "Some men have no sense of self-preservation."

This time, Josh managed to get on his hands and knees. He wanted to stand, dammit. A boot connected with his ribs and his entire body rocked with pain as he rolled onto his back.

*Okay*, he managed to think through the nausea, *this is not the time to struggle. Go limp. Act half-dead. Helpless. That's what Snow wants.*

Snow crouched beside him and brushed hair off Josh's sweaty forehead with one dry, cool finger. "You weren't supposed to see Kir like this. You were supposed to bring him in and say, bye-bye."

Josh experimentally opened one eye.

"We don't like outsiders to observe the inner workings of the agency."

Snow appeared more amused than annoyed, which alarmed Josh.

"But you have," Snow continued. "So you might as well see everything. Sometimes we enjoy an audience. Isn't that right, Kir?"

Josh wasn't sure if the desire to vomit was physical or emotional. All he knew was he wanted to get the fuck out of here.

Snow rose and moved away. "All this distraction, Kir, when I've looked forward to seeing you after our time apart. You've been away from home a year. How are you, love?"

25

Kir didn't move, but a tremor ran through his body. Josh was beginning to understand why Kir killed the men who hunted him, the men who were supposed to bring him in to Snow.

"Thom, tie up Sir Galahad in case he tries to rescue our dear boy." He slapped Kir's buttock. "It's time you came in. A little rebellion and killing are fine. One needs to stretch one's wings. But enough is enough."

Kir reacted with the shakes and Snow looked upon him with a fondness Josh found repulsive.

"I don't have more cuffs," said Thompson.

"Use rope, whatever. Just do it right." Snow indicated a cupboard and Thompson dutifully pulled down a piece of rope. "Truss him up so he can watch. I want audience, not interference. Afterwards I'll reward Kir and let him do what he wants to this good man who risked life and limb today to bring in the rogue Minder. The agency will be very grateful." Snow cast a look of false regret Josh's way. "It's unfortunate Kir has such a powerful temper."

Thompson methodically bound Josh's wrists and ankles so he was hog-tied. Though he could have sat up on his own, he allowed Thompson to prop him against the wall. Best to act helpless when he'd just managed to slide a knife out of Thompson's boot and up his own sleeve.

"Done?" asked Snow.

"Yeah." Thompson sounded bored. "Can I go?"

"What? You don't want to watch the show?"

"Not particularly."

"Shut the door on your way out." Snow turned back to Kir. "We didn't need him anyway, did we? He doesn't appreciate you the way Josh and I do. I can see you've kept yourself in good physical shape. Not that I can speak for your emotional state. We'll have to explore that."

Kir just hung there, breathing loudly under the black hood. Maybe this was one long panic attack for him.

"Okay. First things first," continued Snow. "Let's administer the good drug. The one that calms you down and tells you to listen to me."

Kir's groan made Snow smile.

"So feisty. I've missed you." He touched the inside of Kir's elbow.

Kir jerked.

"Shhh, it won't hurt. I promise. I know you've been through a tough time, always hiding, always making people ignore you. Well, except for Josh here who gave your bike a flat so he could lead you home. We decided to hire a freelancer since you so easily identify any agent who comes after you. And this ex-marine appeared to have all the right qualifications. Well, except for competence."

Kir bucked again. Josh began to feel he wasn't quite in the room. He was elsewhere, watching a horror show. Not involved. He never had been. Though slowly and unobtrusively he sawed away at the rope with his borrowed knife. The most important thing in his life right now was that knife and the fraying rope. Snow must not notice them.

Fortunately, Snow was more interested in Kir's noises and actions. Like a capable nurse, he tied a plastic band around Kir's arm and waited for the bucking to subside. When it did, he jabbed the needle. Kir tried to twist, but Snow kept a lock on Kir's tense, unwilling arm.

"Stay still so the inside of your elbow isn't one enormous bruise, Kir." Snow pressed the needle home and withdrew it. "I have to give you credit, love. You fight to the bitter end, no matter how hopeless the cause. A bit stupid, but a certain amount of spirit is appealing. Don't you think, Josh?"

Josh met his gaze because he wanted Snow to look at his face, not his wrists and ankles.

"Actually, you look rather disgusted and slightly green," Snow observed. "Don't you like to watch?"

"No." The word was barely audible, caught as it was in Josh's thick throat.

"Kir, Josh doesn't like how I'm treating you. And to think, you are his gift. To me." Snow stroked Kir's arms and the boy trembled. "Nice muscles. I see you've been working out. Lifting weights?" He traced Kir's biceps and moved his fingers slowly over the vibrating skin, lingering in sensitive areas, under the arm, at the neck, circling a nipple.

Kir whimpered and Josh continued to cut his ropes, now working on his ankles.

Snow stopped touching and pulled off Kir's black hood. The boy's face was sheet-white, eyes wild with terror. He pulled air through his nose as if he couldn't get enough. Liquid tracked down his cheek.

"Aw. Always so emotional. Don't cry, Kir." Snow leaned forward to kiss the corner of one eye, but Kir turned away. Snow tsked, tsked, then crooned, "Don't fight me anymore. Come back to me now."

Kir wouldn't look at him. Snow sighed and brought both hands to Kir's head, forcing him to gaze into Snow's eyes.

The rope around Josh's ankles was difficult to cut because of the angle of the knife and the need to hide his movements. But he was going to make it. He just needed a little more time.

"I'm glad this drug works so quickly. It's better when we can talk. And kiss." With that, Snow ripped the tape off Kir's mouth and Kir grunted in pain. Again, Snow caught Kir's face between his two palms and this time Kir struggled. "Calm, calm," said Snow soothingly while Kir gulped air and was anything but.

"I am so very happy to see you again." Snow rubbed his thumbs back and forth across Kir's cheeks.

"Can't. Breathe," Kir gasped.

"Let me help you." Snow's voice was soft and sincere. Kir continued to pull in long breaths, while Snow brought his open mouth to Kir's and kissed him, forcing Kir's lips to meld with his own. Kir tried to move away and couldn't, pinned by cuffs and shackles and Snow's own strength. Josh worked on his ankles. The fucking rope was thick and plastic, but he was getting close.

Snow's kiss was thorough and oppressive and unending. Minutes passed while Snow kissed invasively. One hand reached around the back of Kir's head and dug deep into his thick hair, holding Kir in place, while the other hand roamed the shuddering body. The struggle was painful to watch but it slowly abated until Kir began to moan in distress. His body gradually became limp under Snow's kisses and caresses.

Only then did Snow tamp down the kiss and pull back. "Remember now?" he said softly. "I take the fight right out of you."

Kir panted, as if exhausted.

Snow smiled. "Can't talk? Maybe that's for the best." He traced a tear down Kir's cheek and stroked his jaw while Kir labored to breathe. "See, that wasn't so bad. Just like old times, no? Submission. It's the only way." Snow brought his mouth back for another forced exchange of saliva and just before their mouths touched, Kir went stiff, reared up in the amount of space allowed him, and head-butted Snow for all he was worth.

Josh flinched at the crack. Snow staggered back, reeling. He pressed a palm to his forehead and managed not to fall over as he leaned against the wall. Snow took a couple of minutes to recover, then looked at Kir.

"You stupid little fuck." His voice was vicious. "Is it pain you want?" Snow glanced at Josh who remained expressionless, hands and wrists in position, then returned his furious gaze to Kir.

Kir smiled back sleepily. "How did I do that? I'm on the good meds."

"Shut up." Snow walked over and slammed a fist into Kir's face. His head whipped back. Kir's body went slack.

"Maybe it's time to visit your backside, eh?" Snow let the sentence hang there in the room while Kir stiffened, his face turning white again.

Snow's smile turned ugly. "Honestly, what did you think? But that's the problem, you don't think, you just act. You need to leave the thinking to me."

Kir shook his head.

"Good boy." Snow patted Kir's shoulder. "No words. That's the first step. But I do have to punish you. You've been quite naughty. I won't rip you, though God knows you deserve it. I'll play with your asshole and soften you up."

Snow grabbed Kir's hair, pulling his neck back at a painful angle so he could stare down at him. "You want me to fuck you."

"No." The word was hoarse. In this position, Kir's throat was extended and the swallow obvious. Snow pressed a hand against that long column.

"Did you just try to force me away?"

"No!"

"Because I'm strong, remember? Stronger than your words." Snow's gaze didn't leave Kir's face as he squeezed the boy's vulnerable throat. "I'm going to fuck you hard. And despite all these denials, you will come. Because you love it up the ass, even if you can't admit it. You're such a mess you don't even know what you want." Kir's tears had started again. "After that, you'll obey me. If you don't, we'll go through it all again. Clear?"

The boy trembled.

Snow rounded the vaulting horse, finally turning away from his audience, and Josh moved. Four long strides—they seemed to take forever—as he crossed to Snow. Then Josh was behind him, jamming an arm under Snow's chin, setting the knife against his throat, cutting skin. He wanted blood, badly.

Snow froze, swearing under his breath.

"Move your hands and you are dead," Josh promised. "I may be freelance, but I am not unskilled."

"Wow. I'm impressed. Are you this susceptible, or were you primed?"

Josh ignored the question. "*Now.*" The word vibrated with emotion. Josh couldn't quite stay calm, but he didn't care as long as the knife remained at Snow's throat. "We are going to slowly walk over to the wall, and you'll put your hands up so they're nice and safe."

"Yes. Of course," said Snow.

"Kill him now, Josh," shouted Kir, his voice hysterical and compelling. Josh pressed the knife deeper. Blood began to flow. He checked himself, unsure.

Snow elbowed him, going for his own weapon, and Josh made the decision to kill. The knife slipped. Josh slid in just above the collarbone, pushed up, slicing through cartilage. The throat opened, blood spurted and Josh shoved the body away

31

as it fell. His head roared and, for a moment, he couldn't think with the noise of it.

He backed up. The world moved in slow motion as he tried to process what he'd witnessed and what he'd done. And why? Kir's words echoed in his head. But Snow had gone for his weapon and Snow would have killed him.

Still, he was in a room with a psi who could open his mouth and force Josh to act against himself. Who was restrained but not muzzled. Slowly Josh turned to face the beautiful, abused monster. Kir had twisted his neck to watch Snow die and now he watched Josh, his expression blank, his face drained of color. Josh needed to get away before Kir spoke. But Kir's words came at him and all he could do was brace himself for their impact.

"You must help me escape."

# Chapter Three

Kir and Josh stared at each other for a very long time. The boy's face was almost gray, except for the purpling bruises on his left cheek and forehead.

Josh's thoughts danced about, as if they could evade the power of Kir's words. Words that could pounce on Josh's mind and twist him to shreds. Josh wanted to flee but Kir's dark gaze held him until Josh realized Kir's expression held no expectations. The boy simply endured.

In the end, Josh couldn't bear to see Kir bound like this, caged in this room. It felt all wrong. Josh could not walk away.

"Let me get those shackles off you."

Kir exhaled one long breath of relief. "The key's on the side table."

"Side table. Right." Josh went and picked it up. Just before he reached Kir, he stopped. He had to say something about the role he'd played in Kir's capture. "Look. I didn't know you'd end up like this."

"No? You thought Snow was going to, what? Treat me like a human being and not his beast? He's my handler, you know."

It hurt to look into Kir's melting brown eyes. Josh bent over to work on the first cuff, avoiding Kir's gaze. "This is all going into my report and it's going to go back to the agency and it's going to go high."

"Go high?" demanded Kir, amusement lacing his slight hysteria. "They won't listen to you. They *are* high. Untouchable."

"My contact has connections." Though Horton wouldn't necessarily use them.

"So does Snow's boss. Your report will go exactly nowhere. Believe me, my welfare—or yours for that matter—is the last thing the agency cares about."

"Christ." Josh released Kir's right wrist and gazed at the scraped, bruised skin. "We should treat that."

"Never mind." Kir laid his freed hand on Josh's forearm. It was an odd, forced gesture. Josh glanced from Kir to his hand and back to Kir again. "Josh, right?"

He nodded.

Kir swallowed. A fine sheen of sweat broke out on his face. "You have to help me escape the agency."

"You've said that before."

"Yes." Kir looked like he was about to pass out. "I get repetitive and weak when Snow drugs me. When I need to be clear. Sorry."

Josh didn't know what to say. He couldn't hand Kir over to another Snow. But he also had a responsibility to society at large.

"Escape," repeated Kir, his dark gaze potent. He gripped Josh's arm hard enough to bruise.

"Okay," said Josh without thinking. He stared at Kir, then at the key in his hand. He wasn't quite sure what he was doing, though it was obvious Kir needed his help.

"Josh?"

"Yes."

"Are you okay?"

"I don't know. I don't like it here." Such stupid words coming out of his mouth. What was the matter with him? He always knew what to do. One of the reasons he was good at his job. He made a decision and went with it.

Josh rubbed a thumb against his temple. He'd lost his train of thought, but Kir was still bound to the fucking vault horse and Kir had to escape this loathsome place.

"So you'll help me escape?"

Josh eyed Kir suspiciously. But it was a question, not a directive. "Yes." Josh immediately felt better at this decision. "I will."

"Thank you." Kir's complexion had become alarmingly gray.

"Are *you* okay?"

"It's been a shitty day, all in all."

"Do you want to unlock your left arm yourself?" Josh's proximity seemed to unnerve the boy. He jumped every time Josh inadvertently touched him. But when Josh handed over the key, Kir's hand shook so badly he couldn't free himself.

Josh retrieved the key. "I'll do it."

By the time Josh was working on Kir's ankles, Kir's teeth were chattering.

"Are you going to be sick?" asked Josh.

"I think I'm in shock," Kir managed to stutter.

Once Kir's limbs were free he sank down beside the vault, unable to do more than wrap his arms around his legs and rock back and forth.

Josh walked over to pick Kir's clothes off the floor, then crouched down beside him. "Kir?"

Kir looked at him but the boy seemed far away, in pain.

"You need to get dressed. Someone from the agency could come here at any time. And we still have Thompson to deal with."

Kir nodded and took the clothes with shaking hands. He fumbled with his boxers, barely able to get one leg through.

Josh wondered if Kir was having some kind of fit. "Do you want me to help you?"

"You won't hurt me, right?" Unlike earlier, Kir's gaze was diffuse and his voice fainter. The plea made Josh wonder about Kir's fabled powers. As far as he could see the boy was vulnerable and helpless.

"No. I won't hurt you."

"Thanks."

"For God's sakes, don't thank me," Josh said harshly and Kir stared at him in a strange kind of wonder.

*Shock*, Josh told himself. Kir flinched at Josh's touch, but Josh got him dressed. Kir went back to huddling on the floor when Josh stood.

"I need to take care of Thompson before we leave." Josh armed himself, somehow feeling better able to deal with Thompson than this psi-boy who'd been, in times past, raped into submission.

As Josh slowly eased his way into the rest of the house, he soon discovered Thompson was gone. After double-checking that the house was empty of anyone but Kir and himself, Josh stood in the living room, trying to connect the dots. He was, by and large, considered clever. Right now he felt stupid.

Perhaps Thompson had allowed Josh to lift a knife off him. At the time Josh couldn't believe his good luck but now he had to wonder. With Thompson gone, he and Kir were free to leave, which was too good to be true, yet absolutely necessary.

Josh rubbed his forehead, as if that would bring clarity. It didn't. Panic threatened. He took a deep, calming breath and clamped down on his whirling thoughts. When all else failed, it was time to turn to instinct.

Today instinct screamed at him to help Kir escape. With that decision made, he grabbed a blanket from one of the bedrooms and returned to Kir who hadn't moved.

Josh wrapped him up. Cold and pale, Kir didn't react to Josh's touch.

"Thompson left," Josh said. "Isn't that strange? It doesn't fit with what I understood of his character."

Although Kir looked at him, he didn't seem to hear, lost as he was in his own hell. Josh picked him up, carried him to the garage and placed him in the passenger side of the SUV. Getting behind the wheel, Josh drove to his own car, a nondescript vehicle parked a couple of blocks away. They transferred to the Mazda, Kir stumbling from one vehicle to the other.

After Josh put on Kir's seat belt he settled into the corner of the seat, as far away from Josh as possible, watching without, Josh felt, seeing. The boy's face was ashen with exhaustion, his bruises a stark, brutal contrast.

If nothing else, the boy was too sick to manipulate. That thought set Josh at ease. "Where exactly should we go? I haven't run before."

Kir actually paid attention to the question. "East. I know someone in Atlanta."

As good a place as any, Josh figured. By the time they reached the highway, Kir was sound asleep.

♋ ♋ ♋

Kir woke disoriented. His head was killing him, perhaps literally. He didn't have an unlimited ability to use his "magic", as Thompson had called it. Minding took its toll.

He'd forced Josh to run with him and he wasn't at all certain he'd been clever to do so. Except he had been in no shape to run alone. They'd have caught him in some state of collapse, and life with the agency would have started up again.

Josh glanced over and jabbed a thumb backwards. "Drink."

Kir dragged his body up and halfway over his seat to reach the stash of water bottles in the back seat. With unquenchable thirst, he gulped, grateful it was dusk and the bright light of day wouldn't hurt his tired eyes. Everything about him was tired.

God, he'd been out for hours. "How's the gas? I need a pit stop."

"We can stop." Josh looked at him with real concern, or perhaps concern manufactured by Kir. Josh had no reason to care. *Pathetic, to force someone to care about you.* For a moment Kir feared his self-loathing would rear up and grab him by the throat and he'd be unable to breathe.

Instead, he rinsed his mouth with water, leaned far out the window and spat. As if water would get the taste of Snow out of his mouth.

"I don't know what I would have done if you hadn't woken soon," said Josh. "Your deathlike trance is rather disconcerting. Now you're getting some color back."

"Today set me back some." Let Josh believe all of Kir's weakness was due to Snow. Let Josh forget that Kir could manipulate him. Let Josh never know that manipulation cost Kir physically.

"I was thinking of taking you to the hospital."

Kir shivered. "I'm glad you didn't. I'm fine, really."

Josh looked dubious.

"I've been worse." Kir attempted a game smile.

"God." Josh shook his head. No doubt about it. Josh's pity was working in Kir's favor.

"I'm sorry I can't spell you."

"You're sick."

"Yeah, but I don't know how to drive either."

"I know," said Josh.

"The files."

"Yeah."

"What else do the files say about me?"

Josh didn't answer right away. If Kir had been stronger and if Josh wasn't already confused enough by Kir's work, he might have insisted on an answer. Because knowing what the enemy knew would be valuable. But he needed Josh to keep his head on straight and that meant no more magic for now.

Josh pulled off the highway. Then, to Kir's surprise, Josh answered his question. Kir wasn't used to answers freely given. Of course, he wasn't used to spending time with anyone either.

"The file says you have a sister." Josh sounded curious.

*Maddie*. His destination. Kir tried to keep his voice level. If they knew anything about Maddie's current status, he might as well be dead. "Do they say anything about her?"

"Only that she disappeared when you were twelve."

That hurt still, but he didn't want Josh to know. "Anything else?"

"No, except there was a picture," Josh said. "Out of date, no doubt. She doesn't look like you."

"She's my half-sister. Her father was a redhead. I was conceived in India when my mother thought dragging my sister around to different wisemen would solve her problems."

"You never heard from your sister again?"

*Yes.* "No." Kir sometimes wished he hadn't. Maddie ran with the other Minders and they were cruel people. Well, so was he, as Josh would find out sooner or later. Just not yet.

They turned onto a side road and made their way to a gas station. As they pulled into the parking lot, Kir examined Josh. His profile was attractive—square chin, now stubbled, strong nose, firm lips. A man's man. Kir had been surprised when he'd picked up vibes on the bike trail. Then again, his radar was totally out of whack.

Josh stopped and pressed both hands against his eyes. The poor man was tired from the drive and from doing as Kir ordered.

"Thompson came in incredibly useful today. He gave me unmarked cash in an envelope, I borrowed his knife and he disappeared." Josh rubbed his forehead, unable to make sense of today's events, because of Kir whose magic was Josh's poison. Kir silently promised to manipulate Josh as little as possible. "Convenient, don't you think?"

"Very." Kir couldn't explain that his sister had primed Thompson to set Kir free if Snow was ever to trap him again. But he offered Josh an explanation, so Josh could let go of the conundrum. It helped that Kir spoke the truth. "Thompson actually despised Snow."

"I can understand that."

"Can you? I don't think you do understand. He despised Snow's sexuality. If I'd been a woman, he'd have been fine."

# Chapter Four

"How old are you?" Josh knew the answer but banal conversation might help ease the tension in the car. While Josh had driven through the night, Kir had slept. He no longer seemed like the walking dead, just sickly and scared.

When he wasn't sleeping, he watched Josh.

"Age?" prompted Josh, so he could think of something besides Kir's unsettling gaze.

"Twenty-two, as I'm sure they told you. How old are you?"

"Twenty-eight."

Kir looked him up and down. "Do you have a boyfriend?"

The question surprised Josh. He didn't imagine Kir would be much interested in his love life. "Not at the moment. You?"

"Very funny."

"Is it?"

"I've never had a boyfriend. Just couldn't find the time. Too busy being a freak."

Tension wafted off Kir.

"Actually, I lie. Snow was my boyfriend. But you killed him." Kir was striving for flip, but the tremor in his voice ruined his attempt.

Josh drove silently, not sure how to handle that comment, and finally managed, "I think you can do better than Snow."

"Limited opportunity. Snow brought me up."

"Shit," Josh muttered helplessly.

"How many boyfriends have you had?"

"Serious boyfriends?"

Kir shrugged. "However you count them. *I* don't know."

"Four serious relationships. Lots not."

"How many not?"

"I don't play the numbers game." Josh had given out enough information.

Kir stared out the window. "Just curious what normal life is like. That's all. I don't generally get to talk to one of the masses."

"I'm not sure I qualify as normal. Kir," Josh redirected the conversation, "I think we better stop for food, though there are some bagels in the back."

"I lost my appetite yesterday."

"Eat to keep up your strength. You look like death warmed over."

Kir obeyed. Again. The irony didn't escape Josh. Kir was supposed to be scarily unmanageable yet he did as he was told. Maybe when he got his health back things would change.

"So, when will you use your magic on me?" Josh had meant the question to come out lightly, but the words didn't allow it. In fact, he hadn't a clue where those words had come from. He'd been thinking about bagels. His heartbeat got funny and he had an unusual panicky feeling.

"I thought I wouldn't." Kir slowly chewed his mouthful.

"You killed others who tried to bring you in."

"You're not bringing me in now, are you?"

Josh shook his head. He couldn't. Not after yesterday.

They drove in silence for another half hour, until Josh pulled off the highway to buy gas and hamburgers. They ate in the car, Josh hungrily, Kir dutifully.

"Are you nice to your boyfriends?" Kir asked out of the blue. "I mean," he laughed, embarrassed, "do you care about them or is it just, you know, physical?"

"Could we stop talking about my sex life?"

"Yeah, sure," muttered Kir.

Josh glanced over. Kir's face was unevenly flushed and he seemed younger than his twenty-two years. Josh sighed. "Why are you so curious?"

Kir fidgeted. "I know, the pickup was fake. But I keep thinking about it."

"Oh." Josh turned back to the road. Under other circumstances, he would have been gratified that a hot younger man wanted him. But yesterday, and the part he'd played in Kir's capture, rather put a damper on things. "I think we'd better talk about where we're going, instead."

ᦔ ᦔ ᦔ

By the time Josh paid the motel owner and entered the dingy room, he felt like he was moving through molasses. He'd driven for more than twenty-four hours and his time was up. His limbs were exhausted and his eyes wanted to close, despite his fifth shitty cup of coffee for the day, this one from a machine. He wouldn't have lasted another hour on the road.

Kir looked at the room in dismay.

"What's wrong?" asked Josh.

"There's only one bed."

"That's all they had. Sorry but I'm not searching for another motel. I'm too far gone. You can sleep on the floor if you're bothered. I'm honestly too tired to do anything, even if that was my intent."

"I know that." Kir hunched over, as if Josh could never be attracted to him.

Josh dragged himself to the bathroom for a shower and crawled into bed. Vaguely aware that Kir was settling down on the floor, Josh fell deep asleep within minutes.

Much later, he woke to silence. The clock's red numbers showed three forty-seven a.m. For a moment he thought Kir had taken off. He couldn't see him on the floor and he certainly wasn't on the bed with him.

He turned over and saw the boy sitting crunched up in a chair watching Josh in the gray night. As if Josh were the cause of his vigil. Kir's dark eyes were black, his pupils large with lack of light.

Sitting in the chair was doing Kir no good, especially after his gray-faced day on the road. And while Josh wasn't his babysitter, he felt, after the run-in with Snow, responsible. Josh propped himself onto one elbow. "Hey."

Kir nodded, uncertain.

"There's enough room for two to sleep here."

Kir seemed to shrink.

"I'm not going to rape you."

"I know that," Kir rapped out, but his leg began to jig.

"Do you?"

"Yes."

Josh reached a hand out, palm up. "Okay, give me your hand."

"I don't like touch."

"Try it."

The boy scowled and Josh said, "It's just a hand."

Kir stared at it, as if mesmerized.

"We need to sleep," Josh explained. "If I'm going to help you, I'd like to do it properly. Trust me here."

Kir took a breath and leaned over, slamming his hand down on Josh's so hard it stung. Josh clasped his fingers around Kir's, watching him the entire time.

"Who's the last person to hug you?" asked Josh.

"Snow," Kir spat. "He liked hugging."

Kir's whole arm shook, yet he didn't pull away.

"Snow doesn't count. Further back."

Kir swallowed. "Men. Strangers who wanted sex."

Josh wondered how Kir had managed, though maybe he'd been in better shape than now. "Any non-strangers?"

"My sister. Before they separated us."

Josh remembered. "Madeline."

A sheen of liquid covered Kir's eyes. Josh tugged on his arm gently to encourage Kir to come to the bed.

They stared at each other across the darkness.

"Be brave, Kir. You need to sleep."

"I can't." The two words were a plea.

Josh tugged again.

Very carefully, Kir climbed down from the chair and into the bed. Josh backed up to give the boy more space. Kir's movement was awkward, but he got under the covers and lay down at the very edge. Josh allowed a body's width between them so he wouldn't crowd Kir. Across the space their hands remained linked. He liked Kir's hand. It was blunter than his

46

and slightly wider. Colder, too. The boy had become chilled, sitting in that chair.

"Close your eyes," Josh said.

"I don't think I can."

"It's easy."

"Nothing is easy."

Josh saw the telltale glisten of tears. As if stillness could hide their existence, Kir didn't move.

"You've been through too much."

The tears ran and Kir made no noise at all. With anyone else, Josh would have pulled them close, but he merely held that hand.

After a while Kir mumbled, "I can't sleep here with you. I don't know why I thought I could. I want to. Sitting, I think too much, and the floor's uncomfortable." He wiped his face. "And you're nice. I'm not used to nice people."

"Just lie there, see what happens. It has to be better than that chair."

"I can't get Snow out of my head," he rasped, his panic rising. "He was always touching me."

"Did you ever touch Snow?"

"No! Not for years."

Josh let go of his hand. "Touch my face."

"Your face?" repeated Kir, incredulous. But he froze and his breathing got loud.

"If you want," Josh added. "I won't touch you."

It took Kir a while to move, but eventually his palm came down on Josh's cheek. The hand shook, but stayed.

"Sorry I haven't shaved."

"I like your face." Kir sounded shy.

Josh smiled.

Kir palmed Josh's jaw and neck, then stroked his shoulder before trailing fingers down Josh's arm until they clasped hands again.

Kir breathed more easily.

"I'm going back to sleep now." Josh could no longer keep his eyes open. He half-expected Kir to retreat to the chair but Kir was gripping his hand as Josh fell asleep.

When he woke in the morning's light, Josh was facing the wall. It took him a moment to remember why he was in this cheap room that smelled faintly of smoke and cleaning agents.

*He was on the run with Kir.*

That idea was too strange to process. He wouldn't run with a Minder. They were genetic monsters. Even frightened ones like Kir. *Especially* frightened ones.

Very slowly Josh turned around. Kir was on the bed, backed up to the edge. He'd pulled himself into a quasi-fetal position. His knees almost touched Josh.

Josh didn't know what Kir's files were missing, but they were obviously missing too much. That Snow was a rapist. That Kir was terrified.

His long eyelashes were swept down, resting below his eyes. For some reason that made Josh's chest ache. As desire washed through him, Josh closed his own eyes for a moment. It was so wrong to want Kir, especially under these circumstances, but Kir's stark beauty invited seduction.

The boy's eyes flew open and his body tensed up. In one movement, he pushed himself up and off the bed to standing. Josh had the impression Kir didn't recognize him.

"Hey Kir," he said softly.

Familiarity lit Kir's eyes. "Josh." He uttered the name with relief, which Josh found gratifying.

Josh slowly sat up. "That's right."

Kir eyed the bed with some uncertainty.

"We were tired," Josh explained. "We slept."

"Yeah, I know." Kir nodded a few more times. He seemed embarrassed as he rubbed the back of his neck. "I'm not used to spending this much time with one person. It's kind of weird."

Kir's loneliness cut Josh. Kir must have seen something of it on his face because he ducked away and padded off to the bathroom.

After he disappeared behind the door, Josh glanced around the room and took stock of the situation. He was immediately assailed with doubts about the wisdom of what he was doing. If nothing else, he was setting himself up for a very long prison sentence. Yet, there was no way in hell he could hand Kir over to the agency. After Snow it was simply impossible.

*Murderous.* The word shocked him as it came into his mind unbidden, as if the memory of Kir's violent history had been hidden by fog. How could he have forgotten Kir was wanted for murder?

Maybe they were lies, the files, the videos he'd watched. Everything. The boy seemed too vulnerable, nothing like the sullen version they had on file. People had hurt Kir when they shouldn't have.

Still.

Josh's head began to throb as he circled around these thoughts again, unable to bring any kind of coherence to them. He had to sit down. *Vulnerable. Murderous. Minder. Snow.*

"It's after nine," said Kir, emerging from the shower. Josh looked up at him. "We'd better—" Kir stopped. "What's wrong, Josh?"

Josh pressed the heels of both hands to his temples, as if that would create order in his head. Nothing made sense anymore.

"Josh, no," cried Kir in dismay.

Josh locked fingers over his forehead. "What am I doing?" he asked himself.

Kir knelt at his feet. "Look at me."

Josh did. Though he might drown in those eyes, he didn't want any harm to come to Kir.

"Why am I on the most-wanted list, Josh?"

"You killed agents," he said tonelessly.

"Two agents. They were going to take me to Snow, if they didn't kill me first."

Josh remembered. Last year, Kir had used his magic to elude the agency. "You got one of them to kill his partner and himself."

"They gave me no choice." A pleading note had entered Kir's voice, but it didn't erase Josh's fear, or confusion.

"What is my fate, Kir?"

"I like you."

Josh dropped his hands and laughed. "You *like* me? What the fuck does that mean?"

Kir looked away, uncertain, and suddenly, despite Josh's head pain, the other portrait of Kir snapped into place. The lost abused boy. The beauty.

Snow's blow to Josh's head, as well as twenty-four hours of driving, had done little for Josh in the way of clear thinking.

Very tentatively, Kir laid a hand on Josh's arm. The boy lifted his face, ready to speak. But instead, he closed his mouth and laid his forehead on Josh's knee.

Josh ran a hand over the thick, unruly hair and Kir breathed a sob of emotion.

"My head hurts like hell, Kir, and I don't know why."

"I'm sorry," Kir whispered.

"It's not your fault."

"I don't like the killing." Kir spoke to Josh's feet. "That's my problem. I don't like the magic, either, but I use it when I have to."

"Kir."

Kir raised his face. His eyes were dry but pooling with emotion. Josh could lose himself in those liquid brown eyes.

"I am going way out on a limb for you," said Josh. "So don't lie to me and don't use your magic on me."

Kir started kissing Josh's palm. Josh, shaking him off, stood. "What are you doing? You could barely share a bed with me last night."

"I was scared."

"And you're not now?"

"No."

"Why not? Nothing you say or do makes sense." Josh's voice rose and his head throbbed.

Kir stared, his gaze became more intense, and suddenly Josh understood that he was under Kir's sway. "*Don't,*" he yelled at the boy.

Kir flinched but he didn't look away. "You will help me get to Atlanta because you *know* I only kill in self-defense."

Josh stared at a silent Kir and couldn't remember what they'd been talking about. All he knew was the conversation had been heated, which wasn't good for Kir. The boy was always so pale. Josh feared Kir might faint. "Are you okay?"

"Yeah." Kir appeared drained, almost defeated. He swayed before sitting on the edge of the bed. Pointing to the bathroom, he said, "Your turn."

"Right." Josh walked into the dingy tiled room. At least his head felt all right. He'd been worried yesterday's long drive would give him a killer headache.

When Josh came back out, Kir was still sitting on the bed, unmoving, hollow-eyed despite a night's sleep.

"Ready to go?" Kir asked.

Josh nodded.

# Chapter Five

Wrung out after manipulating Josh, Kir slept in the car for most of the day. He'd hoped not to work on Josh again. It made Kir sick to hurt Josh, who had eased him to sleep last night. Kir didn't know the last time someone had held his hand.

He needed to leave Josh whole.

Through his eyelashes, Kir watched Josh drive steadily over the endless highway. Their time together was almost over. Maddie was coming for Kir and he would never expose Josh to other Minders. Josh was good and kind and had the clearest gray eyes Kir had ever seen.

And would see no more. In another world, he would stay with Josh, not with a sister Kir didn't fully trust. But he was here and now, and he did not belong with Josh who deserved better than a Minder who used him.

Josh glanced over. "You awake there?"

Kir opened his eyes in answer.

"At least your color is back. Why do you always look so sick?"

*Because I'm using you.*

Josh waited for an answer and Kir shrugged. He could not explain anything, couldn't even express his gratitude, couldn't say, *I will die if the agency gets their hands on me again.*

"Well, I'm glad you're better now."

"Thanks," Kir mumbled. They drove through the rest of the day silently.

By the time they were ensconced in their next dingy motel room for the night, Kir had recovered. Knowing it would be over by tomorrow evening—he would slip away from Josh who would later thank God Kir was out of his life—made him restless.

Josh showered while Kir zipped through channels with the remote. Nothing caught his interest. When Josh came out of the bathroom, he walked over and stared down at Kir, as if ready to talk.

Kir didn't want to talk. He sat on the edge of the bed, bouncing slightly, wondering if Josh could see right through him, see the poison as well as the desire.

"Can you turn off the TV?"

"Sure." Kir did.

"Thanks." Josh settled down on the other bed. He'd made a point to get a room with two double beds this time, even though now Kir wanted to share sleeping space, and more. "Kir, we had better discuss our plans. Or lack thereof."

Briefly Kir closed his eyes and prepared himself to steer Josh away from this conversation. Because if Josh thought too hard he would realize—again—that his actions made no sense. At least for a law-abiding citizen who worked for the agency.

"We're doing good." *Weak answer.*

Josh shook his head. "Blind luck. Someone must be chasing us."

"We don't have to worry."

"Uh-huh. Why aren't you looking at me, Kir?"

*Shit.* Kir rummaged in the grocery bag and pulled out the bottle of wine he'd bought.

Josh sighed.

"You don't like wine?" Kir unscrewed the lid of the cheap wine and poured a glass. He raised the bottle towards Josh.

"I don't drink."

"Why not?" So much for distracting Josh with wine.

"I just don't like it. Besides, right now I want to think clearly."

"I don't," Kir muttered, lifting the motel's plastic glass to his lips.

"You know the agency has been pretty careless about you."

Kir looked at him over his glass, trying to figure out what would convince Josh to leave the subject alone.

"Speak, Kir," Josh demanded.

"Thompson helped us." That much he could say.

"Thompson *helped?*"

"Yeah. He owed me one."

Josh snorted in disbelief. "He wouldn't care if he owed you one, or not. He's a shit. No way did he help you."

*Not without some encouragement, no. Maddie got to him.* "So Thompson loses his job. Maybe he wanted out. Whatever. He let us get a good jump on them. By now, after three days drive, we could be almost anywhere in the country, no?"

Josh backed up to the headboard, stretching out his legs. "Doesn't sound right."

Kir gulped wine. He would not, he *would not*, push Josh. But he had to do something.

"Take it easy on the wine," Josh told him. "You were pretty shaky earlier today."

Kir downed the rest of his glass.

"I can see you're in the mood to listen to me," Josh drawled sarcastically. "Are you in a rush with that wine?"

"Sort of." A wave of intense emotion hit Kir, something like grief. He was going to miss this person who cared about how much wine he drank. Because that concern came from Josh himself, not Kir. "We'll separate in a day or two. I guess that will be a relief for you."

A frown settled on Josh's face. "I'm not sure. I don't know what I think of this misadventure of ours."

Kir poured himself more wine, looking for courage. "At the park I was really happy when you invited me back to your house."

"I'm sorry about that."

"I hadn't spoken to anyone for a long time, especially not someone who was interested in me." Kir darted a glance at Josh. "Were you interested in me?"

"Kir, come on." Josh's smile was lopsided. "I'd studied you for a month. Of course I was interested in you."

"That's not what I mean. I thought," Kir took a fortifying breath while his heart hammered at his admission, "you were attracted to me."

"You are attractive," Josh said matter-of-factly.

Kir waited for more, holding Josh's gaze. When he said nothing, Kir swallowed bitter disappointment. He could not possibly seduce Josh. Kir controlled minds, but did not wield charm. There were Minders who forced desire and sex upon normals, but long ago Kir had vowed never to sink to Snow's level. And to damage Josh was unthinkable.

Josh crossed his arms as if bracing himself. Subconsciously he knew what Kir could do. Breaking eye contact, Kir placed his elbows on his knees and his head in his hands.

"I think you're trying to distract me." Josh's voice was rich, soft, beautiful and Kir closed his eyes. "The question is why."

Josh hoped silence would prompt the boy to respond.

Abruptly, Kir stood, removing his shirt to reveal well-defined pecs and abs. Okay, not quite the desired response, though not without a certain appeal. However, Snow had made certain Josh knew Kir had a great body and the thought of Snow had a rather dampening effect.

Kir looked at him for approval or encouragement. When Josh gave neither, his expression became almost mutinous and he pulled off his jeans.

Josh's cock hardened though he tried not to show he was affected. He was noticing all the wrong things—Kir's rounded shoulders, brown nipples and dark, curling chest hair.

Kir's expression turned stubborn and uncertain. A charming combination, alas.

"You could hardly hold hands last night," Josh pointed out.

"I'm calmer today. And you don't seem to mind me like some men do."

"Mind you?"

Kir's gaze slid away. "My jumpiness puts some people off."

"Your fear, you mean."

Kir glared. "Do you want me or not?"

"It's just not a good idea."

Kir looked at a loss. "Why not? Unless you're just looking for an excuse."

*Joely Skye*

"I don't need an *excuse*, Kir."

"Nah. I'm a freak."

"You're on the run. You've been abused—"

"Abused! Just fuck off, man. I don't want your fucking pity." Kir shrank back into the chair and tried to pull his shirt back on. After several attempts his shaking hands balled the fabric up and he threw it away in disgust.

Okay, so Kir wasn't exactly an expert at seduction. Well, that was a good thing.

"When did you last have sex?" Josh asked.

Kir's gaze burned. "Doesn't matter."

Josh waited.

Finally Kir blurted, "Six months ago."

"What happened?"

"Met at a bar. I got drunk enough. Went to the toilets."

"What did you do?"

"He fucked me."

"Did you like it?"

Kir shrugged, shivering, perhaps from cold, perhaps from the conversation.

"Before that, when did you have sex?"

"It doesn't matter." Kir's voice went a little high.

"It matters to me."

Kir swung his gaze back to Josh. "Why?" he asked furiously. "What are you trying to prove? That I'm worthless? Trash?"

"I'm not trying to prove anything." Josh gestured rather uselessly. "It can be good to talk, you know." Though talk wasn't on Josh's mind. He wanted to show Kir good sex—when it wasn't forced, or sordid.

58

Kir stretched out his feet and placed them on Josh's bed. He stared at his toes. "I went back to some rich guy's hotel room," he said, as if by recounting these trysts he would change Josh's mind. "He wanted me to suck him off but I wasn't any good so I offered him my ass."

"I think I see a pattern here. Are you offering me your ass?"

By now Kir's teeth were chattering, but he nodded anyway.

"Christ, Kir, get warm at least. Get into bed." Josh pointed to the other double bed. But Kir looked so forlorn Josh shifted over and lifted his blankets. "Get in here," he said with some resignation.

Kir glanced up, hesitation and hope warring, and he dove in beside Josh.

"You're breaking my heart a little here, Kiran." Josh couldn't help himself, he stroked the boy's hair, his cheek. "Did you ever cuddle with any of your hookups?"

Kir talked to Josh's ribs. "I don't seem to attract cuddlers. I've only cuddled with two people in my life, that I can remember." Kir moved closer, so his face and forearms pressed against Josh's side, but he didn't reach across for a hug.

"Who?"

Kir groaned. "Don't ask. If we talk, we won't..."

"The thing is, I think we should talk, not fuck."

Kir shook his head vigorously and Josh stopped stroking Kir's hair.

"Do you want to be my psychologist? Is that it?" Kir asked. "Psychology won't solve my problems." This was patently true. "Or are you just looking for excuses?"

Josh burst out laughing. "I don't have to look for excuses, Kir. They're right here, shouting at me. We're in kind of a difficult spot. I'm having trouble forgetting it. You've got one doozy of a history—"

"That I want to forget."

"Sex isn't about forgetting."

"It can be."

Josh rubbed his forehead.

"I guess I'm tainted, eh?"

"Stop that," snapped Josh.

"Kind of off-putting to have sex with someone who's been with Snow for more than ten years." Kir vibrated beside him.

"Aw, shit." A sucker punch of emotion hit Josh in the gut and it wasn't desire. Unable to resist the urge to comfort, he slid down beside Kir and pulled the trembling boy into his arms. At the contact, Kir's breathing became uneven and Josh stroked his neck and back, murmuring reassurance. After a while, the boy seemed to relax a little, though he was still stiff in Josh's arms.

"You got too cold," Josh said. "Your fault for sitting around half-naked."

Kir snorted.

Josh kissed Kir's forehead. "How can you make love when you're panicked like this? I couldn't."

"I haven't made love." Kir spoke into Josh's shoulder. "But sometimes, when I had sex, I'd stop thinking. It was the greatest thing." He was panting, just a little. Josh's cock lay against Kir's stomach, Kir's against Josh's thigh. They wanted each other and they were both hard, despite the rather damping conversation. Josh hadn't meant to get in this deep. Despite his honorable intentions, it seemed cowardly to extricate himself right now.

"I'd stop thinking about Snow," Kir clarified. "Sex with someone besides Snow pushes him away. That's why I want it. And I like you," Kir added quickly. "You're *nice*. You have no idea how rare nice is."

Josh didn't know what to do. Though talk of Snow softened his desire.

Kir felt it. "I'm sorry. I say the wrong things."

Josh pulled back. "Hell, Kir, don't be sorry."

Kir leaned forward and awkwardly kissed him on the mouth, before ducking back against his shoulder.

Josh continued to caress the boy. Kir's skin vibrated slightly, but he didn't resist touch. Josh liked the firm muscle that lay just beneath.

"What are you thinking?" Kir asked.

Josh hesitated before answering. "You have a beautiful body and someone should learn to love it."

Silence.

"I wish we had more time," Josh admitted after a while. "But we don't and I kind of need to understand how Atlanta is going to save you."

More silence.

Finally, Kir said, "You want me to talk, right?"

"Yes." Josh kept the doubt out of his voice. He was pretty sure Kir wasn't going to talk about Atlanta.

"Snow started kissing me when I was ten."

*Hell.* Josh pulled Kir closer.

Kir spoke quickly, a little breathless. "He'd kiss me and open my mouth with his and tongue me and I'd sit on his lap while his cock—though I didn't realize it at the beginning— pushed against my buttocks. The first time I didn't know what to do and it seemed to last forever and I felt kind of weak after. It was punishment. Because I was supposed to convince some old guy to give Snow money, but the guy resisted which meant my magic—as you call it—would hurt him. So I didn't."

Josh kissed Kir's wet eyes, his forehead, his smooth, newly shaved cheeks. Soft, pure kisses.

"I kind of liked it, too," Kir recalled. "Even if it was disgusting. Because no one touched me by then. I was such a freak and they'd separated me from my sister before she ran away. Snow asked me afterwards, did I like it, and I said, yes, and he said, he knew I would. After that, he'd invite me to climb on his lap at the end of every session. I always did and he'd hug and kiss me until I felt kind of sick."

Josh stroked the shivering boy and made soothing noises while Kir clung to him, his heart racing. With his shakes, Kir's touches were tentative and clumsy at first. But after a while the movements became smooth and Kir was bold enough to slip a hand under Josh's T-shirt.

"I like your skin," said Kir.

"Thank you."

"I guess that sounds stupid."

"No." Still holding Kir, Josh asked, "Why are we going to Atlanta? You try to distract me every time I ask that question."

Kir slid down and kissed Josh's stomach.

"Kir," Josh warned.

Kir stared at Josh's chest. Josh could see the sweep of his long, dark eyelashes.

"Well?" pushed Josh when Kir didn't answer.

"I could tell you not to ask me questions."

Josh felt a little cold. "You could, could you?"

Kir balled one fist. "But I don't want to. It's better if you don't know when they catch up with you." He raised his face to look at Josh, his expression pleading for understanding.

"If you don't trust me, Kir, why are you in my bed?"

"Come on. You know what they're like. They'll drag that knowledge from you."

Kir's hand traveled up Josh's torso until his thumb touched Josh's nipple. Josh trapped that hand.

"Believe it or not, I'm trying to protect you, Josh."

"But how are you going to protect yourself?"

A shadow crossed Kir's face.

"Do you have somewhere to go?"

"Yes."

"Your sister," Josh guessed.

Kir didn't answer. He just stared, his eyes dark and unblinking.

"She'll be able to help you?"

"I think so."

"That's not as strong an answer as I'd hoped. They didn't have much information on her in your file."

"She's my best bet," insisted Kir.

"Okay." But the subject had brought back some of Kir's shakiness and Josh didn't understand why. "You don't trust her." His heart sank for Kir. "Isn't there anyone you can trust?"

Kir moved so he crouched over Josh, one hand on his shoulder, while he lay the other hand on Josh's cheek. Kir gazed down at him without speaking. Yet Josh felt that Kir was saying, *you.*

Josh slowly brought Kir's face to his and kissed him, closed mouth, lips soft, tentative. They breathed each other in.

Kir's tongue traced one corner of Josh's mouth. Digging his hand into Kir's hair, Josh pulled him down and took over the kiss, stroking Kir's tongue, tasting wine. Kir threw a leg over Josh's hip, struggling to get closer.

They kissed. Kir's fingers dug into Josh's biceps, as if he feared Josh would rise and leave. Between Kir's grip and his hungry mouth, Josh was losing control. He wanted to flip Kir on his stomach and fuck. Abruptly Josh broke off, turning so he was above Kir.

Kir gazed up in confusion.

"Hey." Josh cupped his cheek. "I'm not going anywhere. I'm here. Just give me a minute."

Kir dashed a hand across his eyes. He was breathing hard again. Josh placed a palm on the boy's chest to feel Kir's heart pounding. His eyes opened to search Josh's face.

"What did I do wrong?" Kir asked. "I wish I had time to learn about you."

"Hell, you did nothing wrong. That's not the problem," Josh assured him. Kir lowered his gaze, eyelashes blocking Josh's view, but not before he'd seen the hurt.

Air baled out of Josh's lungs and his jaw tightened, but he couldn't back off. He slid his hand over Kir's stomach, under the boxer's elastic and wrapped his fingers around Kir's cock. He gasped.

"Okay?" Josh squeezed lightly. The boy was painfully hard.

Kir nodded.

As Josh touched Kir's wet slit, Kir reacted by lifting his ass off the bed. In one quick movement, Josh divested Kir of his boxers, running hands down Kir's strong thighs and calves. Kir jerked one leg still caught in the fabric and Josh grabbed the ankle.

"Stay still," he ordered and Kir's eyes widened. "You don't have to take me so seriously," Josh added more softly. "I'm just getting these out of the way." As the boxers hit the floor, Kir laughed a little shakily.

Josh ran a hand back up Kir's calf, thigh and caught Kir's cock again. He was thick and lovely, with curling black hair and a full sac.

"You're beautiful." A line formed between Kir's eyes, as if he was baffled by the compliment, so Josh crawled over to kiss him lightly on the lips before trailing kisses down his neck.

"Want a hickey?"

"What?" asked Kir.

Had the boy never laughed in bed? Probably not.

Josh's tongue found Kir's erect nipple and caught it between his teeth.

"Oh God." Kir shuddered and Josh played with his other nipple, then made his way down, dipping his tongue in Kir's navel before he came to his cock.

Josh licked him clean and took him to the back of his throat.

"Josh," Kir whimpered.

Josh didn't answer as Kir hardened to steel. He didn't think Kir's cock could take in more blood. Cupping Kir's sac, Josh began his strokes but before he developed a rhythm, Kir spurted. The boy was fast. As Kir pulsed, Josh made love with his mouth. He swallowed, enjoying the taste of Kir—salty, no sourness.

Kir. Who was his target. They were hiding out in a cheap motel room.

*What the fuck am I doing?* Josh raised his face. On elbows, Kir gazed back, anxious, this side of cowering, and Josh's gut twisted, remembering Kir's ugly past. Josh had miscalculated, despite his best intentions to be generous, to show affection.

He sat back on his haunches and opened his arms. Kir hesitated, then bulldozed into Josh, almost knocking him off the bed. Kir's arms came around his neck and under his armpit in a convulsive embrace. They rocked together silently. Josh's throat tightened, his eyes stung.

"Nothing like this before," Kir declared fiercely into Josh's neck. "You remember this is new to me."

"Okay." Josh tried to gentle Kir's body.

"Nothing. *Nothing* like this."

"Hush, babe," murmured Josh. Kir relaxed in his arms and Josh kissed the top of his head.

Kir spoke into his ear. "I'm glad you want me, too."

Not sure what to say, Josh shivered as Kir licked his neck. Kir disentangled himself from Josh and slid fingers down his chest. Josh's face heated up. He caught Kir's hand against his stomach. "That was about you, Kir. Stop now."

"You are the best person I've ever met." Kir's fervor embarrassed Josh.

"Don't be ridiculous."

Kir's eyes shone, as if he had complete faith in anything Josh could ever do and Josh found himself blushing.

"I don't want to stop. You know that. Right?" Kir searched Josh's face, vibrating as he waited for a signal to continue. Josh released Kir's hand.

Josh's dick bucked when Kir touched its head. A drop of liquid seeped out. Kir's thumb swept it up and he licked off precum. He smiled at Josh, the sweetest smile, as if pleased by the taste of Josh.

"You're turning me on," Josh admitted, stating the obvious.

"I'm glad." Placing hands on Josh's thighs, Kir bent down.

He licked Josh's head then took Josh deep, as Josh had done to him. It was awkward but pleasant. Kind of hot, actually, if only because Kir was so eager. He cupped Josh's balls. There was uncertainty in Kir's touch but not quite inexperience. Josh stroked behind Kir's ear, caressed his neck, gave him encouragement.

"You're so good," said Josh. "So lovely."

Kir looked up at that, his eyes black with desire. "Take me."

Josh frowned.

"I want it, especially if you'll hold me." Kir reached into a drawer and pulled out a box of condoms. Well, someone had been prepared, certainly not Josh who watched Kir rip open the square packet, slide a condom down Josh's length and apply a generous helping of lube. The entire prep time, Josh didn't move, immobilized.

Kir turned. Of their own accord, Josh's hands lifted to palm Kir's ass and thighs, stroking the young, firm skin dusted with lovely dark hair. He leaned forward and kissed Kir's spine, up and down the column, tracing the small dips and rises, tasting Kir's sweat.

"Sure?" Josh said.

Kir took one of Josh's hands and brought it to rest on his hard, slick cock.

With his free hand, Josh traced a finger down Kir's spine, between the cheeks. He thought Kir might jump but he moaned when Josh gently circled the muscle. He wanted Kir ready so Josh grabbed the lube and and came back for some finger play. Kir pushed back against him and Josh slid a finger in.

"I'm ready," whispered Kir.

Josh kissed Kir's neck before setting his dick against Kir's hole and the boy said, "*Yes.*"

Gripping Kir's hips, Josh eased in, letting the muscle stretch slowly. Kir pulled in breaths, hissing through his teeth.

"Okay?" Josh shook, ready to ram it home. He had to be patient.

The boy rumbled with pleasure. Slinging an arm under Kir's chest, Josh held tight as he pushed deeper and Kir accommodated him. He ran a hand over Kir's vibrating skin. Josh balanced on the exquisite knife-edge between desire and restraint before reaching for Kir's cock.

"Hey." Kir sounded dazed as Josh traced the heavy vein.

"This is quite the rebound."

"Huh?"

"You're so hard."

Kir groaned as Josh slid his hand up and down Kir's cock. "I think you might come again, Kir. Is that possible?"

"Jesus," swore Kir. "I want *you* to come."

Josh laughed and Kir relaxed enough for Josh to fill him to the hilt.

"Kir?"

"Ungh?" managed Kir.

"You okay?"

"God, yes."

"Then come." Josh bit down on Kir's shoulder and, shuddering, Kir pulsed into Josh's hand. He didn't know if it was youth or excitement or Kir's nature to come so readily.

Kir trembled. "Fuck me."

Josh pulled out and thrust into Kir's warmth, then plunged again, aiming deeper.

"*Josh*," Kir repeated, pleading, encouraging.

"I'm here." The world fell away until there was only Kir with his dark, beautiful body and his light moans of pleasure. White light danced before Josh's eyes and he stiffened.

"God!" he said through gritted teeth as he drove home, pulsing inside Kir whose muscle clenched the base of Josh's dick. He fell forward, but held himself so Kir wouldn't collapse. He blanketed Kir, keeping the contact.

It wasn't the hottest sex ever, but Josh felt quite emotional. He rubbed his face against Kir's sweat-slick back. He was supposed to protect the boy, not fuck him in the ass. Where the hell was his head? Well...

Carefully, he withdrew and sat back, pulling the boy against him, a kind of apology in his touch as he rubbed Kir's shoulder and gathered him into his lap. Kir curled into him, showering his neck and collarbone with kisses, his face wet but his body languid. The trembling had finally ceased and, while flushed, Kir was breathing normally.

"It feels right with you." Kir seemed amazed and grateful. "Special."

"It was special." Josh didn't know what to do with Kir's gratitude so he just held Kir.

"I was hoping..."

"Hoping what?"

"That you would remember me with a bit of love." With that, Kir clung tighter and Josh caressed his back, trying not to be alarmed by this talk of love.

"Don't forget, okay?" Kir muttered against his skin. "Don't forget this was right."

Josh kissed Kir's forehead, because he couldn't find words. He padded off to take care of the condom.

# Chapter Six

In the middle of the night, Josh became sleepily aware that he was holding and being held. Kir pressed soft kisses against Josh's chest and shoulders. His cock stirred and he managed to regret the exhaustion that overtook him as he fell back to sleep.

He was smiling.

Next, he woke with a vengeance. The door flew open, light flared and Kir screamed. Josh's first impulse was to block Kir from the intruders' view. He moved to stand in front of the boy. He wished he wasn't naked but soon had bigger concerns. Someone marched over and placed a gun to his head. Cocked it. Thoughts of nudity fled and Josh froze, holding his breath.

"Speak." The gunman talked over Josh to Kir. "And this guy is history."

Josh couldn't turn but he heard Kir's ragged breathing. No words though.

Josh swallowed. "Can we get dressed?"

"Slowly, carefully. You first."

Josh retrieved his jeans and shirt and refused to succumb to the shakes. He was aware that someone had taken Kir off the bed, but he couldn't see what they were doing to him.

To Josh's relief, the gun disappeared. A man stepped forward and cuffed Josh's hands behind him. "You'll come with me."

Josh turned to see Kir standing half-dressed and shaking. His mouth was taped and Josh's gut twisted. Did they always do this to him? Kir's frantic gaze landed on Josh as if he wanted to tell him something with his eyes.

Josh was pulled out of the room and pushed into a car.

The next few hours passed in a blur. The police drove him to the station and left him alone in a room with occasional visitors who wouldn't answer his questions about Kir. Josh found it hard to track time, especially with that last vision of Kir in his head. Above all else, he'd wanted to keep Kir from harm.

"You should worry about yourself instead," one stranger remarked as he removed Josh's cuffs.

Another came in and asked if he understood how lucky he was.

Josh guffawed, then felt stupid at his loud, uncontrolled laughter. "Lucky? I don't feel very lucky at the moment. I feel like shit."

"Most people don't survive contact with a Minder. You seem to have forgotten that they mess you up, buddy."

"Kir didn't."

"That's what they all think. Until they're dead."

"He didn't," repeated Josh, wishing he wasn't arguing with some cop who knew nothing about Kir and psis. *Kir has a crush on me*, he could have said, but Josh wanted to keep that information to himself. Even if he and Kir had been found in the same bed.

"No." The cop's tone suggested just the opposite. "He didn't work on you at all. He was desperate and you just agreed to run away with him."

*You didn't see what they did to him.*

The cop hiked up his pants. "Let me ask you a question. Are you normally attracted to men, or just Kir?"

"I'm gay," Josh said flatly, but his heart began to race. He recalled that he had not intended to have sex with Kir. His face heated up, thinking about last night's intimacy. But the idea that Kir had forced the sex didn't make sense because earlier Kir had been genuinely frightened. That had been no act. Snow's viciousness had been real. Josh wasn't so confused he had made up Kir's past abuse and present skittishness.

"I hope so, for your sake. Because these fucking Minders, they plant illusions in men's minds."

*Not Kir.* But his head hurt and Josh pressed the heels of his hands against his temples.

The man stared with some satisfaction. "Your contact wants to talk to you."

Josh blinked at the cell phone offered to him, then picked it up. The cop left to give him some privacy.

"Horton?"

"Josh! You're in one piece?"

"Yes. I'm being held at a police station in Fairview."

"Good."

Josh didn't feel good.

Horton continued, "You're safe and while you've broken all kinds of laws I think, under the circumstances, you won't be punished too badly." He paused and when Josh didn't respond, he added, "I'm flying in with the agency. We'll take care of you."

"Okay." But Josh's heart sank, thinking of Kir and what they would do to him. "Make those agents go easy on Kir."

"Go easy?" said Horton, incredulous. He cleared his throat. "Don't worry, Josh. Kir will be properly taken care of. As will you. No one is blaming you. We understand what Kiran Brunner is. You were putty in his hands."

Josh felt lightheaded. "Oh yeah?"

"We don't have to talk about this now. In fact, it's probably a bad idea. But you should know that we're on your side."

"Why do you think I was manipulated by Kir?" Josh should shut up. He wouldn't do himself any favors by insisting on his autonomy. But he couldn't stop himself.

"Josh." There was pity in Horton's voice. "It's on tape. Kiran Brunner ordered you to kill Snow, and help him escape."

Pain throbbed in one eye and Josh pressed it. "Snow was going to rape Kir. Did you get that on tape?"

Horton paused. "We shouldn't talk about this now, Josh. Later."

"Did you see, *on tape*, what Snow did to Kir?" Josh insisted, his voice rising. He had to get himself under control but pain pulsed through his temple.

"Snow's relationship with Kiran Brunner will be investigated," Horton said placatingly, as if Josh had lodged a complaint about the dress code. "Perhaps the relationship had become a little warped. But we can't be sure that's all Snow's doing. They think Snow lost control at the end to Kiran Brunner."

"So Snow could rape him? Like hell." *You didn't see him last night.*

"Josh." That voice full of pity again. Josh wanted to smash Horton's face. "Kir is one of those Minders who use sex to manipulate people. Just be glad you got out alive."

"Oh, I'm glad." He wanted to throw up. Instead, he turned off the phone and put his head between his legs. The problem was, he couldn't remember what was real right now. Kir had yelled for him to kill Snow, but by that time Josh had had no choice. He thought.

And last night, those emotions had felt real. Surely Kir didn't shake and tremble on cue?

Josh stood and walked around the room, shaky himself. He tried the door but it was still locked. He leaned his forehead against the cool wall, trying to remember when Kir might have ordered him to have sex, or make love or feel real affection. But Josh knew enough about Minders to understand he wouldn't necessarily remember that. They made you forget you'd been given an order.

It had been Josh's decision to save Kir. Hadn't it?

The door opened and he spun to face whoever was there. He tried to cover his discomposure. A woman stood at the door and she didn't react to his expression. She just pinned him with her brown eyes. "Josh Mackay?"

He nodded.

"Follow me. No questions. You don't want to hurt me."

"Okay," said Josh while his body filled with refusal and denial and fear. But he followed her out like a dog on a leash.

It was early morning now. They took a circuitous route out of the station and passed only one man. "You'll let us leave," she told the guard and he agreed.

Soon they were outside and Josh found it difficult to think.

"Get in the car," she said. "Then don't move."

It was easy to obey.

She walked around the other side and it was only as they pulled onto the road that Josh realized he recognized her. She was an older version of the picture he'd seen in Kir's file. The picture of Kir's sister, Madeline.

He found it hard to breathe and sweat broke out on his forehead. She turned and smiled at him. "Relax. Don't worry."

A strange, iron calm fell upon him. He floated outside his body, watching himself act as Madeline wanted him to act, and he didn't mind. It was, he thought with some hope, utterly unlike his experience with Kir, where he got too involved too quickly.

She drove into the suburbs. Although a different city, Josh couldn't help but think of the safe house he'd taken Kir to a few days ago. She parked in the driveway and got out of the car. Then she sighed and poked her head back in to look at the immobile Josh. "Follow me."

He did.

A girl let them in the house.

"Well?" Madeline asked sharply.

"Kir's here," the girl answered. "Down the hall."

Madeline seemed to relax a little at that. She turned to face Josh who trembled. "Come on."

There was no compulsion behind the words. Josh just stood there, breathing, the vise that had gripped his chest receded.

She sighed again, as if he was a nuisance. "I'd rather not force you to enter the den because you're giving me a headache, but I can and will." She gestured and, after a slight hesitation, Josh followed. Because her orders were making him sick, not because he wanted to see Kir again.

"Bring us some tea," she called, then turned to him. "Do you want tea?"

"I don't know. You tell me."

She smiled faintly. "I'll take that as a yes." She indicated the door to the room. He was to precede her.

"Are you going to lock me in?"

"Worse. I'm going to sit with you."

"I'd rather, under the circumstances, that you didn't talk. It makes me twitchy."

"As you wish. But, after all, you just spent days with my baby brother. You must be used to us by now."

Josh just looked at her, without speaking, and she shrugged.

When the tea arrived, she merely lifted the teapot in question and Josh nodded to receive his cup. He wasn't a big tea drinker, but he was thirsty.

She sat, completely at ease while Josh became more and more tense. "It won't be long now," she said with some sympathy.

Josh didn't answer.

Down the hall, a door slammed. "Get your fucking hands off me." Josh recognized the voice, hysterical, shaky, *Kir's.*

Madeline jumped and strode to the hallway, though she kept an eye on Josh.

At the sound of Kir approaching, Josh felt sick. Basically, he never wanted to see Kir again, yet he didn't know how to reconcile that with his desire to protect Kir.

"Maddie?" Kir sounded uncertain.

"I'm here, Kir," she called. "It's fine."

"It's not fucking fine. I've been manhandled and I can't fucking stand it."

She rolled her eyes. "Get a grip, okay? I just rescued you when your mouth was taped shut and you were trussed up like a chicken."

"*I liked it where I was!*"

"Come here," she said with false calm. "There's someone I want you to see before we all head out."

Silence. Then Josh heard Kir's footsteps. Madeline backed up so Kir could stand in the doorway. When he saw Josh, his angry face went blank.

Which was pretty much how Josh felt. Blank. He couldn't trust any of his feelings. He couldn't look away from Kir either, away from those brown, fathomless eyes. The eyes and voice had made him kill a man. Had made him run. Had made him fuck. Josh had been some kind of automaton. The Minders called those in their thrall zombies.

To Josh's surprise Kir broke eye contact first. Josh had been expecting another order. Instead Kir turned to Maddie.

"*Why?*" he asked, as if she had caused him a great deal of pain. Josh felt even more at a loss.

"So you could say goodbye," she said softly. "Let him off the hook a little, if you care about him."

Kir shivered, then quickly brushed his eyes with the back of his hand. "He's not safe here and *you know it.*"

"I've stayed with him the entire time, haven't I, Josh?" She didn't wait for his answer. "And we'll be leaving soon."

"Why?" he repeated.

She smiled, but the smile was sharp and cold. "They were hurting him there, though they didn't know it, by telling him you'd messed with him."

"*I did.*" The anguish in Kir's voice angered Josh. He was tired of feeling protective about someone who had done him harm.

She shook her head. "You haven't changed. You have to learn when to shut up. And when to speak." She gestured impatiently. "Anyway, I'm running out of time. You have a few minutes to be clear with him, if you choose. You can help him put his head back on straight before you leave him for good."

Kir didn't look at his sister again. He walked through the door and slammed it behind him, shutting Madeline out.

To Josh's dismay, his hand shook when he reached for his tea. He gave up all pretense of control. "Maybe it's better"—he talked through clenched teeth and rage shook him by the throat—"if you keep your shitty little mouth shut."

"Josh—"

"Shut the fuck up," Josh said furiously. "No wonder you don't like touch when you only know how to prostitute yourself. I was already fucking helping you, but that wasn't enough. I had to fuck you."

Kir shook his head.

"Well, say it. Say no and I'll *have* to believe it whether it's true or not."

Kir jammed a hand into his hair, revealing yet another bruise on his face. Bright purple compared to the older, yellow ones Snow had left. For someone who could manipulate others, Kir seemed to invite a lot of physical abuse.

"I wish I could tape your mouth shut now, because I don't want to hear a fucking word you say. Because I don't know what it will do to me. You made me kill someone, Kir. I was your fucking tool."

"He was going to kill you," Kir said dully.

"Oh, I see. You saved my life. How kind. Well, if I don't believe it now, you just have to repeat it again, with feeling."

Kir glared at him, sullen, angry, *lost*. It struck Josh as highly unfair that Kir could look so uncertain.

"Just cut this lost-boy crap, okay? I've had my fill."

In response, Kir launched himself at Josh, as if to pin him to the couch. Josh fell back, surprised by the contact. Then, furious, he knocked Kir to the floor and landed on top of him, knees on Kir's arms. Josh raised a fist above Kir's face. A face discolored by new and old bruises. A face that turned to the side, ready to submit to the blow. Kir's body went limp beneath him.

Josh let his arm fall. "Shit," he said in disgust, wondering if Kir somehow wanted the violence. God knows he couldn't figure out much about the boy.

Josh stood. "Get out."

Kir pushed himself up and scrubbed his face, as if warding off tears. Josh loathed his tears.

"I didn't push the sex, Josh, only the escape."

Josh couldn't believe a word. He clung to that knowledge so he didn't feel crazy.

"I won't forget you," said Kir.

"Oh, great." Josh desperately wanted to forget Kir.

Someone opened the door. A man, tall, hefty, not particularly handsome or athletic. But strong. Kir seemed to shrink.

"We're leaving," the man declared. "Now. So get in your kiss goodbye."

Kir looked down, saying nothing.

"Ah, an unhappy parting." The man eyed Josh and Josh froze. Oh God, not another one. He didn't think he could cope. "I'm Brad. Perhaps you want to kiss *me* goodbye."

Josh struggled, hooked in place, trying to figure out if he wanted to kiss Brad or not. He hadn't thought so until Brad smiled.

Kir announced, too loudly, "I'm coming."

Kir moved away from Josh and went to Brad who circled an arm around Kir's bowed shoulders. Brad caressed his face and Kir submitted to it. "Welcome home, love."

"Let's go." Kir took the man's hand, pulling him away from the threshold. He turned to close the door and Kir's face was blank again, his eyes hollow, and Josh found that yet again he wanted to rescue him.

The door shut and Kir was gone.

Josh sat alone with his tea and tried not to think. He didn't move for the longest time. But the last scene kept playing itself in his head—Brad's hand on Kir's face and Kir's submission. Something about a kiss. The last few days made no sense and his mind was falling apart. He wasn't even sure how he'd gotten here.

They said this happened when Minders worked too hard on someone. They broke down and sometimes never came together again. So Josh just stared at his cold tea and occasionally sipped it.

Eventually it occurred to him that he heard only silence in an empty house. He was alone. Hard to imagine why he was here. He ventured out of the den to find a telephone. He figured he should phone his contact. At least he could remember Horton's name and number.

It didn't take long for the police to arrive, with Horton and another agent in tow. Horton couldn't seem to get over Josh's survival. Not once, but twice, Josh had escaped from the clutches of the Minders. People just didn't do that.

Horton stopped talking when Josh no longer tracked the conversation. Josh thought he slept then. He didn't remember much, just that time passed. He found himself in a hospital, sleeping a lot, with occasional visits from Horton and the other agent, Walters. Sometimes they came together, sometimes separately. Horton became his interrogator.

Too often, Josh dreamed of Kir and he became enraged by his desire to see the boy again, to ask him, *why*? No explanation could be trustworthy but still, Josh had to dream it. It was an exercise in futility. The yearning made him weep.

He told no one. Not that there was anyone to tell but Horton and Walters who continued to visit; the agency allowed no one else in. After a time, Josh realized they wanted something from him—his memories. It took days for him to make sense of his time with Kir and when he did, Josh couldn't differentiate the real from the imagined. Presumably Kiran Brunner could have suggested every memory, every moment— was anything he remembered real?

"No," said Walters when Horton put forth that theory. "Minders push people to do things and that can result in false memories, but it's not so common. If Josh, for example, remembers staying at a motel, they almost certainly stayed at a motel. We've tracked them now, anyway."

"I remember lots of things." Josh remembered killing Snow, he remembered driving a heck of a lot, he remembered making love. The last was most painful because he had cared, as if he were falling in love, which didn't make much sense in hindsight. Josh didn't fall in love in three days with some skittish colt of a boy who was, in fact, faking it the whole time. Josh closed his eyes, remembering Brad's caress on Kir's face.

That was the problem. He couldn't make sense of Kir's actions.

"Josh." Horton was annoyed by Josh's lack of focus, but conversation was difficult to follow.

"What I don't understand," Josh said finally, after their third round of going over all the details of his encounter with Kir, "is why Kir wasn't with his sister and her gang from the beginning. Why he was all alone when I lured him to the safe house?"

"Well," said Walters, as if he didn't know how much to say. "We don't understand the Minder society all that well, but they appear to prey upon themselves. The younger, weaker ones don't fare that well. Maybe Kir didn't like it there."

"His sister couldn't protect him?" asked Josh.

"Like I said, we don't understand them well." Walters went silent and looked out the window.

Horton was less circumspect. "Why are you crying? Kiran Brunner is still a threat to us all."

Josh placed an arm over his eyes to hide his tears, but still he spoke. "What will happen to him?"

"We don't know. They occasionally kill each other." Horton was unaware of the pain he caused Josh, or perhaps didn't care. "I'd guess his sister will look out for him. We'll catch him if we can. Catch them all, if possible. We think there may be twelve of them."

*Twelve.* And Kir had avoided them all.

"You shouldn't care," added Horton. "He used you."

"Yeah," said Josh with disgust, but he couldn't decide where his disgust was directed. He just remembered Kir clinging to him after sex, talking about love in an eager, unabashed way which had nothing to do with Minders and zombies.

Josh tried not to ask the question, but it came out despite himself. "Will you let me know if you find Kir again?"

Walters looked away while Horton took his time answering. "Josh. We *will* find Kiran Brunner again and we'll need your help."

Josh shook his head. "I can't go through this a second time."

"You have no choice, Josh. It's that important."

Josh didn't speak. There didn't seem to be much point. He could, perhaps, argue against it later.

And he did, but by that time he was living in a secure compound with severe restrictions and no one had any intention of listening to him.

He'd been hired to capture Kir and somehow he'd ended up the prisoner.

# Zombie

# Dedication

To my editor, who makes each book better. Thanks for your support and hard work, Sasha.

# Chapter One

Josh Mackay had an escape plan. It would take time, patience and technical know-how, but he had those ingredients. He just needed to create opportunity.

Not that he was a prisoner, oh no. The agency even had a job for him. Though he could never work in the field again— Horton worried about his ability to withstand stress. Josh had swallowed that line at the very beginning, but he'd long been aware the agency simply didn't intend to lose the one man who'd survived his time with a Minder. They still asked him questions about Kir, though the long sessions with the psych had finally ended.

Josh rubbed his temples. The headaches were apparently a consequence of his time as a Zombie. A fact he should have believed and didn't quite, because his headaches were weather related and had been since he was a teen. Today was overcast and the barometer ran against him.

This reasoning, he'd been told, was denial. Or the power of suggestion. The Minder's power was large and all-encompassing and if Josh sometimes remembered Kiran Brunner as vulnerable, he no longer shared that opinion with anyone in the agency. They gave him pitying looks when he suggested Kir wasn't pure malevolence.

Josh sighed. It had been two years since he'd been abducted by Kir. If he'd ever been grateful to escape with his mind intact, that gratitude had been chipped away by the agency that had taken control of his life by imprisoning him in this compound.

Oh, they gave him a "home"—his little box of a house furnished by someone else—and he'd become quite good at keeping the compound's computer hardware up and running. But the lack of choice sometimes grabbed him by the throat and shook him with frustration.

Plotting his escape kept him sane and gave him a future. He wasn't in a rush. He had to do it right or he'd end up back here, under stricter surveillance. Taking on a new identity was a tricky business.

He would miss his half-brother, though they rarely chatted. The agency didn't want a hotshot young lawyer nosing into agency affairs. Josh's mother was dead. His father was not interested in the son from his first family. His friends didn't know where he was.

The agency thought he blamed Kir, the Minder who'd made Josh his tool. Under Kir's influence, Josh had sliced open a man's throat and run from the law. He'd also fucked Kir. That it didn't feel like sexual abuse, then or later, just made it all the more twisted. Or so the psych had said.

Josh pulled out some aspirin and popped them in his mouth. Aspirin, the cure-all for psychic pain. Or pressure headaches.

Someone knocked at the door.

"Yep," called Josh, expecting Horton who visited Josh twice a week. Duty—Horton had recruited Josh for the Kir job—made the visits dull. But Josh didn't entirely discourage them. He was isolated and needed some kind of socialization.

He looked up and was startled by the appearance of someone new. *But not quite new.* The shock of recognition was a physical reaction that left him breathless as the man's blue eyes pinned him to his chair. *Move before he speaks,* his brain screamed, and Josh wrenched away from that gaze, twisting as he reached for the emergency button.

The man said, "Don't touch that."

Josh hesitated and stared at the black circle that would summon help. His fingers were inches away from the smooth plastic. *No rash decisions.* If he made a fool of himself the agency would watch him even more carefully and he'd never escape.

"Why don't you look at me," the man suggested.

Josh obeyed, turning his chair to stare up into the large blue eyes of...*Brad.* One of three Minders Josh had met in his life. An acquaintance of Kir's.

"I'm no threat to anyone here," Brad assured him. "Relax."

Josh shook in the chair, his body straining, but to do what he wasn't sure. Brad was a large guy and strong, his expression friendly and patient. A memory flashed, of Brad caressing Kir's face and Kir enduring it. Josh shuddered as he tried to be calm. The agency didn't like hysterics.

"We've never met before today," Brad said.

Josh felt his eyes widen and he really looked at the man this time. The stranger reminded Josh of someone, but wasn't that often the case.

The man walked over. "I'm new here. Brad Carlisle."

Josh rose and gripped the proffered hand, trying not to be repulsed by someone who was pleasant-faced, well-dressed and polite. "Josh Mackay."

"I've heard a lot about you." Brad didn't release his hand.

"You have?"

"You're quite the survivor."

"Thank you." To his amazement, Josh blushed, and he didn't know where the emotion came from because he sure wasn't attracted to this guy. Even if his heart was racing.

Brad placed a large palm against the back of Josh's clasped hand. He stood there, rooted to the ground, unable to move, his one hand caught between Brad's two. Josh was embarrassed.

Brad couldn't help but notice. He smiled. "Settle down. I know what you're feeling."

As if hypnotized, Josh stared into those eyes. The blue was like crystal when Brad concentrated.

"Lust." Brad identified Josh's reaction. "It's taken you by surprise. You've never been this strongly attracted to anyone."

Josh's throat went dry, his head roared and he couldn't think straight.

Brad released him. No longer smiling, his gaze was intense. Josh couldn't stop staring. His chest hurt.

To Josh's relief, Brad stepped back. "Well, I'm sure I'll see you around."

Josh jammed his damp hands in his back pockets and nodded. "I hope so," he said fervently and blushed again.

"You're cute." With a disarming grin, Brad left the office.

Josh slowly shut the door. Air whooshed out of him as he bent over, hands on knees, breathing hard, as if he'd run ten miles on a full stomach. He was so nauseated he might vomit. Instead, he gulped air until the nausea subsided. Shakily, he sat back down in the chair and stared at the tiny camera in the corner of his office, the one that monitored him constantly. Right now he hated it. He'd felt an overwhelming attraction to a perfect stranger. The intensity was unprecedented. To his shame, his strong reaction was caught on video.

He would figure out how to get Brad alone, off-video. Brad had been interested. Now thirty, Josh hadn't been cute for years but he was willing to be anything for Brad.

*Brad.* The name echoed in Josh's head and all he could think of was Brad Carlisle.

A while later, Josh looked at the clock, appalled to find he had done nothing but stare into space for almost an hour. He scrubbed his face, panicky, because self-discipline and concentration were vital if he was to escape this compound.

*There's no rush.* Josh wanted to get to know this new guy. He'd fantasized about Brad for that lost hour, though now Josh couldn't quite pin down a specific thought. His mind had been a cloud of lust.

He hadn't crushed on anyone for a very long while and never so quickly. Well, captivity had done little for his sex drive and there just wasn't much opportunity to meet anyone.

Brad would change that. Josh was so excited by the idea, he felt ill. God, he had to get a grip on himself because he was shaky again.

*Okay, time to go home.* Go for that short walk down the road to his little house in the compound. There were other houses, but people didn't live here unless they were imprisoned like him.

And no one was like him.

Maybe Brad would visit. Josh looked forward to it.

♋ ♋ ♋

Josh didn't sleep well, perhaps because he forgot to eat, perhaps because his headache started again and this time hurt like hell. At three in the morning he lay down and closed his eyes—after he'd spent the last hour doing something he'd sworn he wouldn't do again.

He'd sent a message to Kir.

Short as always, though the why of it, now that the message was gone, was difficult to comprehend.

By morning, the agency would be delighted. After all, they hunted Kir, in life and on the internet. But Josh's communications with Kir had not given the agency what they wanted—Kir himself. Instead, beneath what the agency observed, he and Kir had set up a secret correspondence by embedding messages into pictures. It proved Josh had some autonomy and he needed that proof. The leash they kept him on was choking him. He dreamed of suffocation and closed places, and it didn't take a psych to guess why.

In the morning he woke to banging. Someone was at his door. Exhausted, he stumbled out of bed and pulled on his jeans.

"Yeah," he called from the living room. Not that they couldn't have entered without permission. But they maintained the illusion of politeness.

Horton walked in with his sidekick, Daniel.

"Sorry to barge in." Horton burst with energy. "Kiran Brunner emailed you last night."

Kir always responded to his embedded messages. This visit had been inevitable.

"Another picture?" Josh tried to show only the slightest interest.

"A photo of himself."

Josh blinked, surprised. Kir usually sent scenery shots, nothing personal.

"That's a personal touch," explained Daniel, in case Josh didn't understand the difference between scenery and Kir.

"See. I told you to keep those photos going out." Horton clapped Josh on the back.

*You haven't a clue.* But Horton thought his advice to Josh about Kir was invaluable.

"I wonder what prompted him to respond to you last night?"

Josh shrugged, though he knew the answer. Kir only answered when Josh mailed under the agency's radar.

"You'll have to write him back," said Horton. "Try to engage him in a conversation."

"He hasn't written me a word in two years. That's not going to change now. He just likes pictures." In the beginning, Josh had felt guilty for not revealing Kir's words to Horton, when Josh had still thought Horton had Josh's interests in mind. That guilt was long gone. Horton had one goal—to capture Minders—and while he might regret that Josh's freedom had been sacrificed on that altar, he would never let Josh go.

"He hasn't sent you his own photo in two years, either," Daniel pointed out.

"Uh-huh." Josh scrubbed his face. "Do you think I can have breakfast first, while you guys analyze the picture inside and out?"

"May I?" asked Daniel. He pointed to Josh's computer.

"Be my guest." As if he had a choice.

While Josh scavenged for breakfast, Daniel searched Josh's private computer for any and all hints of things Kir. Josh could be grateful Daniel was not as clever as he thought he was. The program Josh had written last night to embed his message in the photo had long since erased itself and its tracks.

"So Josh." Horton's overly casual tone indicated he was going to say something he thought important. "You were up late last night."

"Couldn't sleep," said Josh. "Headache."

"Ah. Any better today?" Horton's real concern just made Josh feel more crazy.

"Probably. We'll see how the day progresses."

Josh made coffee for everyone and Daniel spent an hour at his computer, finding photos, but no messages to or from Kir. Josh wanted to wait until he was alone, but they insisted he come see the picture while they looked on.

He walked over, bracing himself, and there was Kir with his dark eyes, sensitive mouth, wild hair. Still beautiful. A little older perhaps, but with the same sullen expression, as if he didn't like his picture being taken. The photo hurt. Josh had spent too many hours thinking about Kir, his beauty and his betrayal.

"It's a bit of a shock for you." Horton's sympathy set Josh's nerves on edge. "Seeing him again."

It should have been love, thought Josh sardonically, except Kir had been Josh's Minder and Josh his Zombie.

"What should I write back?" Josh shouldn't have mailed Kir last night.

"Psych will let you know shortly."

"Okay."

They stood now, ready to leave.

"I'll come to work after psych calls," said Josh. Psych. Three psychologists and Josh loathed them all.

"If you're not feeling well, you can call in sick," Horton suggested.

Josh snorted. "I'm fine. It's too dull to stay in this house all day."

Horton slapped Daniel on the shoulder. "Let's go. Thank you, Josh." Horton's sad eyes looked up at Josh and Josh gazed back until Horton turned away. *Don't give me your useless pity.*

After they left, he pulled up a chair to his computer to stare at Kir. Then Josh created his program and ran the photo through for Kir's message.

Who would have known that he and Kir had even more in common than their lovely Minder-Zombie bond? That they could both program obfuscated C?

Josh still couldn't fathom why he'd written Kir last night.

*I've met someone. I've never felt like this before.*

Kir's answer was short, almost useless.

*Who? Tell me more.*

Josh rid his computer of the message, his program and any traces of either.

Was it possible for Kir's psi powers to reach out from the computer and *poink* Josh on the head? He was pretty sure such capability was nonexistent. What he didn't understand was why he wanted to connect with Kir after six months of silence.

*Brad.* Josh shivered. Somehow he associated Kir with Brad, perhaps because the last man he'd had any feelings for—even if they weren't his own emotions—was Kir.

Psych phoned up. Josh obediently wrote and thanked Kir for his photo, adding that he looked sexy. Psych was stupid. Nothing would put off Kir more, whatever their fucking profile said.

But later that day, Kir sent another photo, this one of an island.

*Never mind me. Is he sexy? Describe him. What's his name?*

The questions sent Josh into a spiral of thoughtless lust and he got little done apart from another obligatory message from psych to Kir. Some tripe about loneliness. Josh wished he'd never written Kir. The fallout was too aggravating, as he'd known it would be. Next time he had insomnia, he'd be sensible. Last night, sense and thought had been decidedly absent. He needed more sleep. Or a friend.

He traipsed over to his office, hoping a change of scenery would help his state of mind.

Just before supper, Brad dropped by. The sight of the man shocked Josh. His heart clenched painfully. His face flushed bright red and he stumbled to his feet. My God, this was worse than bad, it was humiliating. Gauche. Josh needed to get a grip. His smile was sickly.

Brad watched it all good-naturedly. They shook hands again, Brad invited him to come back to his place, and Josh shut down his computer, trying to ignore the noise in his head, hoping Brad didn't notice what an idiot he was.

"Long day?" asked Brad.

Josh figured he looked tired. "Not really. I didn't sleep well last night."

"No?" Brad's gaze sharpened and, as they exited the building, he added, "Well, I better go easy on you then."

Josh glanced across, unsure of Brad's meaning. He wished he knew what to say. At one point in his life he had been an accomplished flirt.

It began to drizzle and Josh pulled up his hood. In silence they walked to Brad's temporary new home. He was here for some kind of intensive training program. Something Brad couldn't talk about.

When they reached the house and Brad opened the front door, Josh stopped, reluctant to enter. Brad applied pressure to Josh's back and Josh's legs took him inside.

"Hey, it looks a lot like my place. What a surprise," Josh joked, trying to ease the tension shooting through his nerves, making his limbs feel like lead. "I think of the buildings here as replicates."

Brad didn't respond to the stupid observation. Instead, he threw his jacket at Josh. "Hang it up."

Josh stared for a moment and Brad watched him, as if looking for a reaction. But Josh didn't mind hanging up jackets. He found two hangers in the closet and used them. By then, Brad was sitting on the couch, picking up the remote.

"You look like a helpful fellow," Brad told him. "You'd like to get stuff for me."

"Sure." Josh didn't understand why his chest felt so tight.

"Could you throw a frozen pizza in the oven and bring me a beer?"

"Absolutely." Josh found five pizza boxes in the freezer, all the same—Brad must like pepperoni pizza—and he unwrapped one and set it in the oven, put the timer on. He pulled a beer out of the fridge, opened it for Brad and took it to him.

"Hey," said Brad. "You can have a beer yourself."

"No, thanks. I don't drink."

"Yeah?" Then Brad lost interest and went back to watching football. Josh stood, unsure what to do, feeling foolish but not able to sit down. He ended up looking at his feet while Brad ignored him. His mind tripped around in a dizzying fashion until, eventually, the oven bell dinged. Josh served the pizza, brought Brad another beer, and they ate.

Josh found his appetite was poor, though he tried to swallow his slice of pizza.

Brad turned down the volume. "Everything okay?"

"Yes. Fine. Thanks." Josh didn't know what was wrong with him—why his hands shook and his body trembled.

Brad observed it all. "You enjoy spending time with me."

Josh nodded. It was true. He'd been alone for too long. That was why he reached out to Kir at odd moments.

"But maybe that's enough for tonight," Brad continued. "Don't want to move too quickly."

Josh frowned.

"Adjusting to a new relationship and all," Brad explained. "Come here and give me a goodbye kiss."

Josh swallowed. Kissing made him nervous, but excited. That's where the trembling came from. And Brad wasn't rushing him. Brad waited on the couch until Josh's legs took him over and he settled near Brad, not quite touching. Still, Brad didn't move, as if he knew Josh was skittish.

"Some tongue," Brad drawled and Josh stopped thinking. He leaned over and kissed Brad's open mouth, tasting beer and pizza. It was a clumsy kiss that became unpleasant when Brad took control, but Josh found he couldn't pull away. He just endured.

After a time, Brad broke the kiss and smiled, as if pleased with Josh. Twice, he playfully slapped Josh's face so his cheeks stung. Then Brad's hands encircled Josh's neck.

"You're shaking, Josh. Why?"

Josh couldn't think why. He licked his lips and wished Brad didn't understand how uncomfortable and nervous he was. "I don't know," he admitted, ashamed.

"It's new," suggested Brad. "You've been alone too long. You have to get used to the idea of us."

Josh nodded while Brad's thumbs pressed into Josh's throat, so it was hard to swallow. He had the uncomfortable thought that Brad could break his neck.

Under the powerful hands, Josh stayed still. Brad had an erection, making Josh uneasy. He didn't feel ready. In fact, he felt like a caged animal.

Disgruntled, Brad dropped his hands. "I'll let you go."

Josh scrambled off the couch, almost falling backwards.

"You'll come back tomorrow for supper."

"Sure." Josh was already reaching for his jacket.

"Josh?"

"Yes?"

"You don't have to worry about cameras at my place. They don't watch me. You're happy to spend time here, where you're not under constant surveillance."

It was so true. Josh detested those cameras. "Okay. Yeah. That sounds great." He winced. He sounded so banal. So *young*.

"Goodbye." Brad turned the volume back up.

Josh let himself out into the cool evening and walked home, glad the cold rain ran down his hot face.

# Chapter Two

At midnight, Josh found himself standing in his living room. He'd come home and tried to watch some TV, but couldn't settle down. He'd taken a shower, brushed his teeth three times and then apparently blanked out. Because here he was, time had passed, and he didn't know where it had gone.

He pulled off his clothes and crawled into bed, hugging the bedding to himself, thinking, *something is wrong with me.*

Then he remembered Kir had asked if *he* was sexy. *Brad.* Josh's mind shied away from the chaos that was Brad. No matter how attracted, Josh might be wise to avoid someone who made him feel crazy.

He should stop writing Kir, too, in case that contact was messing with his head.

Morning came. Josh rose, exhausted again, but he went through the motions of the day and was grateful he remembered those motions. As the agency's permanent guest, Josh had his difficult days. Nevertheless, he needed to keep his crazy moments to a minimum or he'd never escape.

At five, he was getting ready to go home alone when Brad appeared in the threshold of his office door. Josh froze while Brad's crystal gaze cut through all his thoughts and intentions.

"How was your day?" asked Brad.

"Good. Uneventful." Josh laughed, though he wasn't quite sure why. He must seem awfully stupid to Brad. His face heated up as he remembered their kiss.

"Why don't you come over to my place?"

"Sure."

"You must get lonely."

Josh just looked down.

"Come on." Brad now sounded impatient. "Don't drag your feet."

Josh grabbed his jacket, anxious not to slow Brad down, and they walked briskly to Brad's place. In no time they were at his door and, despite himself, Josh hesitated.

"What are you waiting for?" Brad demanded.

"I don't know."

Brad pulled him inside.

They ate more pizza. Brad drank beer and they barely talked, which was a relief because Josh was making such a fool of himself. He wanted to go home, but Brad might be offended at the suggestion, so Josh sat quietly on the chair while Brad sprawled on the couch. Josh rather liked being ignored. If only he could disappear, which was an odd thought.

At the end of the football game, Brad turned off the TV and looked at him. Josh stiffened. He wasn't used to anyone's attention and Brad had a strong presence.

Brad's smile was slow and sly. "I think you're ready. Take off your shirt."

Josh hesitated, searching for an excuse. He'd lost too much weight this past year, which he didn't want Brad to see. "I'm cold," he said lamely.

"It doesn't matter."

And it didn't, so Josh pulled off his T-shirt, balled it up and held it in his hands in front of him.

"Do I have to tell you everything? Put the shirt down."

"Sorry."

Brad looked at him appreciatively. "Nice chest. A bit skinny, but I like skinny."

"Thanks," Josh muttered, embarrassed.

"What do you like?"

Josh couldn't think what he liked.

"I know what you like. I'll remind you." Brad began to stroke his crotch. With the other hand he unbuckled his belt. Josh had expected something to develop tonight and yet a vise took hold of his chest, making it hard to breathe.

"You like cock. And you want me," said Brad, his gaze a directive.

It was true, yet Josh found it hard to move. He just stared, overwhelmed.

"I've waited long enough. Get on your knees and crawl over here," ordered Brad.

Josh slid off the chair and onto his knees, then made his way to Brad. When Josh was close, thick legs clamped onto his sides, squeezing his ribs. The seams of Brad's jeans rubbed against Josh's skin unpleasantly. He shuddered while Brad watched, smiling. Josh raised his arms, unable to rest them on Brad's legs. How awkward. Josh didn't know what to do. Brad solved the problem by gripping Josh's arms and yanking him close. Josh stared down at Brad's erection—the man wasn't small which Josh should have found sexy.

Yet Josh felt too shy to unzip Brad. He grimaced, avoiding Brad's gaze. "I don't know what's wrong with me. I'm shaking."

"You're stubborn," said Brad languidly, which didn't make sense. Brad sat up straight and pulled down his jeans. His cock popped out. "You'll do exactly what I want here and you'll do a great job of it, too. Because you're my new boyfriend." Brad slid a hand around the back of Josh's neck, caressing while Josh gulped breaths. "Suck me." Slowly but firmly, Brad forced Josh's head down.

Josh closed his eyes and didn't think after that. He didn't know where his mind went during or afterwards, but Brad's words rained down, pushing Josh this way and that.

It wasn't until he was walking home in the drizzle that he came back to himself, confused, upset and very much alone. He hadn't thought he'd feel lonely tonight. After all, he had a new boyfriend. But his chest ached with emotion. Maybe he expected too much with this sudden infatuation, as if a relationship could make him complete when his life was empty.

He wished he didn't feel like crying.

When he got home he was sick to his stomach. He recovered, brushed his teeth and showered. He hoped he wasn't coming down with the flu, though he didn't know how he could have caught it. Everyone around him was healthy.

Looking for distraction, he sat at the computer. Two hours later, he was still there. How could so much time pass when he wasn't even thinking? These lapses in memory frightened him. He jumped when the computer beeped to indicate a message had arrived.

One of Kir's fucking pictures. Horton and Daniel would visit Josh tomorrow. *Fucking Kir*, Josh raged. He didn't want another fucking Horton visit. He needed people to *leave him alone*.

With shaking hands, Josh found Kir's message, if only to get rid of it, get it off his computer. Then he stared at the actual words, trying to make sense of them.

*If I can help you, I will. I mean that. I want you to describe your new boyfriend: name, physical appearance, age, scars. This is very important.*

Josh remembered, with something of a jolt, that he'd sent Kir a message tonight. Right after Josh had sworn he would not mail Kir again. What was wrong with his head? He hoped like hell the message had been properly embedded, hidden from the agency. He no longer trusted himself to be sensible.

Why would he ask Kir, of all people, for help? Psych would have a field day with that request.

Josh plunged his hands into his hair, trying to remember what he'd written, because his computer sure didn't. He gulped air, as if his brain wasn't getting enough oxygen.

Slowly, he programmed his last message to Kir. Because this correspondence had to stop even if Kir had offered help. Josh couldn't remember the last time someone had said they would help him. Certainly more than two years ago.

He dashed the back of his hand against his eyes, furious he was getting maudlin. It was Brad he should confide in, Brad whose house had no cameras, not Kir and his secret, meaningless messages. Still, he wrote Kir back: *Brad Carlisle. 6'5". Blond and graying. Crystal blue eyes that cut.*

He sent it off. Kir in all his freedom could laugh, pleased the man who had tried to entrap him was now himself a captive.

Funny thing was, Josh breathed easier now. He was pathetic. A useless offer of help eased his pain. He crawled into bed and slept dreamless, as if deprived.

♋ ♋ ♋

The next day Josh called in sick and stayed in bed. His rest was disturbed. Horton was excited by the plethora of messages from Kir. Three in two days. He and Daniel couldn't have been more delighted. They were in and out all morning, mildly concerned about Josh's exhaustion. By midafternoon, they left him alone and Josh spent the rest of the day fearing Brad would drop by.

The fear embarrassed Josh. Brad was his boyfriend for God's sakes. Maybe tomorrow Josh would feel differently. He hoped the weariness would pass. He slept all evening and night, and woke once to a nightmare he couldn't remember but left him weak and shaken.

By morning he was wrung out. Perhaps he should ask for a physical, but he didn't trust the agency doctors. What he needed was a normal, quiet day. No messages to or from Kir, and if he wasn't up to seeing Brad tonight, Josh would say so.

Nevertheless at four-thirty in the afternoon, Josh gathered up his stuff and ducked out of the office early. He didn't want to explain his reluctance to his boyfriend. Brad might be hurt. Or talk Josh into socializing when he absolutely wanted to be alone. If he knew nothing else, Josh knew he was safer alone at home.

He was making himself food when someone knocked. His first instinct was to run and hide. What a fucking joke. There was no place to hide. Cameras watched everything. He had to get a grip or he'd turn into a nutcase. If it was Brad, he'd explain he didn't want company.

So he marched to the front door and opened it. Brad stood on his step and Josh's heart began to pound. He'd forgotten how Brad mesmerized him.

"Hey, Josh. I came by your office and you were already gone." Brad sounded disappointed in him.

"Sorry." Josh cast around for an explanation. "I came home early. I'm still tired from yesterday."

"I heard you were sick. You're better now, right?"

Josh nodded.

"Come on over to my place and we'll watch TV."

Josh found he couldn't move. He wanted to go with Brad. Yet he had made a sandwich he should eat.

"You like my place," Brad pointed out.

"True." Josh wrung his hands, unsure what to do. "It's just, I made supper already," he blurted.

Brad laughed. "Is that all?"

Josh felt the fool.

"What's wrong?" asked Brad, ever patient. "You don't seem quite yourself."

Josh couldn't think what was wrong. He'd promised himself a quiet evening at home, but couldn't he change his mind? He needed company.

Brad placed a hand on Josh's shoulder. "Come with me."

It was silly to fuss about a sandwich, so Josh slipped on his jacket and shoes. They walked across the compound. Brad chatted about the end of yesterday's football game. Josh nodded when Brad wanted him to. Then Brad took his hand and led him into his house.

Brad seemed different tonight. Decisive, powerful, a little overwhelming. He gripped Josh's hand so hard it hurt. Josh couldn't think of anything else but the pain, until Brad pointed to a bottle sitting on the coffee table.

"I bought vodka for you, Josh." Brad eased the pressure on Josh's hand, but didn't let go.

"Thank you." Josh was shamed by his breathlessness and his aching hand. "I'm afraid I don't drink."

Brad faced him. "Sometimes you do."

Josh nodded. It was true, though he couldn't remember the last time he'd had alcohol. Brad released Josh's hand. Josh let his arm fall to his side, watching as Brad's palm slowly approached and made contact. Brad stroked Josh's cheek while he tried not to jerk away and didn't quite succeed.

Brad caught Josh's face to hold him still. One thumb slid back and forth across Josh's lips. "Don't say you don't drink," Brad remonstrated. "You may not like beer, but you enjoy vodka when you're with me."

Josh closed his eyes in agreement while Brad trailed a hand down his side to rest on Josh's hip. He felt dizzy.

"We're going to have fun tonight after the vodka. Because God knows you need to relax. You're wound too tight, Josh."

"Sorry," said Josh and winced as his ass was grabbed roughly. He tried not to vibrate under Brad's touch, but it was difficult not to react.

Brad bent towards him, hot air on his face, and Josh knew what was coming. He readied himself for Brad's mouth and he was taken, to be drowned by Brad's strange embrace. Time passed without thinking, a lightheadedness so complete Josh wasn't quite aware of himself until Brad tamped down the kiss.

At the end, he caught Josh's lower lip between his teeth and bit hard. Tears came to Josh's eyes. His lip swelled with blood and Brad grinned, running the pad of his thumb roughly across Josh's bleeding flesh.

"I'll pour you a glass of vodka while you get our food and my beer." Brad stepped back.

"Okay." Josh stood there, stunned and stupid, licking his lip and tasting his blood.

Brad turned Josh to face the kitchen and patted his ass. Numbly, Josh walked over to put pizza in the oven. He returned to give Brad his bottle of beer.

"Sit down at my feet and start drinking," commanded Brad. "You need it."

He needed something. Josh thought he might burst with horror. How could Brad feel desire when Josh felt like this? Hoping the vodka would change what was wrong in him, he gulped a large mouthful. His eyes and throat burned with self-loathing.

Brad laughed. "That's the way. Keep going. Not too quickly, mind, or you'll be sick."

So Josh sipped and Brad watched him, drinking his own beer. Josh rather wished Brad would watch TV instead.

"I like it when you take off your shirt," said Brad.

"Okay." Josh set his glass on the floor and pulled his T-shirt over his head. Brad smiled while Josh shivered. Then the pizza was ready and Josh scrambled to his feet to serve Brad, but not himself. He wasn't hungry and he needed to drink vodka to keep warm. If he focused, then all he thought about was the vodka and the heat flowing through his limbs. Before he knew it, the beer mug of vodka was half empty.

"You're enjoying your drink," Brad observed and Josh had to agree. He couldn't remember why he didn't drink more often. "So take off the rest of your clothes."

Josh stood. He fumbled but managed to undress and fold his clothes in a pile.

"A tidy bugger, are you?" Brad grinned, delighted. He spun a finger in the air. "Turn around, I want to see all of you." Josh obliged. "A bit of a skinny ass, but that's okay."

Not sure what to do next, Josh waited, trembling.

"Finish your drink standing up."

The heat of vodka and something else flushed Josh's skin red. The room began to spin while he concentrated on his drink. He was getting drunk, but he didn't want to spill any on himself or on Brad's floor. So he gulped the last mouthfuls and clung to the empty glass. Brad walked over, relieved him of his mug and set it on the table. Then Brad twisted Josh's left nipple until it hurt. "You like pain, remember?"

Josh nodded and felt like he'd spent his entire dizzy life nodding his head like a puppet whose string was pulled and pulled and pulled. At least the pain let him feel something.

Brad took Josh's hand and together they walked to the bedroom. As Brad undressed Josh stared, unsure what to do. Funny, he used to take the lead. Brad pushed and Josh fell sprawled on the bed.

"Get on your hands and knees," said Brad and Josh didn't remember anything after that.

Hours later, Josh became aware of himself under the shower. Brad's shower. Brad didn't want Josh to go home tonight, wanted him to stay for the weekend. How Josh knew, he didn't remember. Then again, his memory was turning to shit. With painful dignity, he washed and dried himself while Brad slept. He was trembling from cold so it took him a while to put on his clothes.

He stared longingly at the door, but he couldn't leave his new boyfriend. Brad wanted him in bed so Josh walked back down the hall and into the room. Terrified he would wake Brad, he approached the bed with great trepidation. He set himself down gently, grateful the bed didn't sway, and clung to its edge. In this state, he couldn't sleep, but he could go away from himself, to a place where he didn't think.

Two hours later, Josh returned. He didn't know where his mind had been and its absence unnerved him. As did the noises he heard, the noises that had brought him back.

At first, he thought he was hallucinating. Gradually he became convinced people had entered Brad's house. Josh didn't wake Brad. Instead, he watched as three shadows stole into the dim bedroom and surrounded the bed.

*Kill us both.* The thought had Josh gasping in surprise.

"Don't make a noise." The female voice made Josh choke on his fear while he backed up against the headboard.

At the same time, to Josh's horror, Brad bolted up to sitting. "What the fuck?"

"What the fuck indeed," she said. "Brad, love, what *are* you doing in this compound with Kir's Zombie in your bed?"

Zombie. *Minders.* Josh began to vibrate with fear. He couldn't survive another Minder.

"That was two years ago," Brad protested.

"We have a no-poaching rule and you know it. Being spurned in love is no excuse, I'm afraid."

Brad licked his lips. "I was here. He was here. Kir wasn't. That's all." He spread his arms. *"That's all."*

"You lie," she sneered. "You thrive on payback. You want to hurt Kir by taking this guy and making him yours."

Josh didn't quite understand. He scanned the dark shadows, but he couldn't figure out what was going on. Brad was his boyfriend. They were surrounded by Minders.

"We know what you do to your Zombies, Brad."

"I've been very patient," Brad insisted. "I've taken it slow. He's not in bad shape. Kir can have him back."

*Back.* In his terror, Josh couldn't stay still or keep quiet. He hummed, inside and out, the sound going high. Someone crouched beside Josh. A hand reached out to take Josh's ·shaking arm and he flinched. His teeth chattered. A scream built in his chest.

"Not in bad shape." Her voice dripped sarcasm. "He's about to wail, Brad. Shut him up, Kir."

The human form didn't speak. It simply clasped Josh's arm and the touch galvanized Josh. He fought for his life. A third party landed on him. A hand covered Josh's mouth as noise tore at his throat. They pressed down on his face and chest while a needle slid into his arm and still he fought.

But soon he weakened. His arms became heavy to lift.

"Let him go," said Kir, his voice flat. Whoever held Josh climbed off the bed.

"Kir?" Josh no longer cared that he sounded the fool, sounded betrayed. They had him helpless, fearful, drugged. Josh hoped to die.

"Hush." Kir stroked the inside of Josh's elbow, massaging the needle's entry point. "Hush, Josh. It's over now."

Josh passed out.

# Chapter Three

Kir gazed down at Josh who slept the pale sleep of the sedated. He was thinner than Kir remembered, had lost weight over the last two years. The word haunted came to mind, and Kir's chest ached.

Maddie was less emotional. She cast Josh a look of disapproval, as if the man himself was responsible for becoming Brad's Zombie. It was Kir's fault. He hadn't been able to hide his true feelings for Josh from Brad, so Brad had come hunting for Josh. Payback, as Maddie had said last night.

"Why must you always choose dangerous lovers, Kir? First Brad who wouldn't let you go."

Kir turned abruptly away. He didn't discuss his sex life with Maddie.

"And now this Josh is liable to kill you."

"Not if Brad left him catatonic," said Kir grimly.

Maddie shook her head. "Josh reacted last night. He was watching. He even fought you." She paused for dramatic effect. "He'll fight you again."

"I can protect myself."

"Can," Maddie agreed. "But you so rarely do. For God's sake, put on some kind of control before he's strong enough to move."

"I push him now, Maddie, and he might break. He was hard to control two years ago. I had to tell him to help me escape *three times.*"

"Brad didn't have a problem getting him into bed."

Kir's mouth curled in disgust. "Brad is a bludgeon. I wish your pod would kill him."

Maddie's gaze slid away. "I don't like him either, Kir. He didn't treat you well. But we don't kill one another anymore. There are too few of us."

"You should make an exception," Kir urged. "Brad places the rest of us in danger."

"You think the agency wouldn't hunt us if Brad didn't exist? Think again. They track down all kinds of genetic freaks, not just us."

He didn't know what she was talking about. "Who else is there?"

She shrugged. "Rumor has it there are werewolves."

Kir didn't believe it, but he just sighed. Talking to Maddie was one, long argument.

Josh stirred.

"What I should do is leave. One psi is enough to freak him out. Imagine two." She paused. "You can tell him not to hurt you—a small safety cushion so he doesn't stab you in the back. That's all. Self-protection is not malicious or self-serving."

Kir loved his sister, but she didn't care about anyone except her fellow psis. "He's too close to breaking. Can't you understand?"

She held up her hands in surrender. "Okay, I give. Just watch yourself."

They walked to the front door of the cabin. It had been her father's, now bequeathed to Maddie. Only she and Kir knew its location. Out in the country, down gravel roads, Kir figured he and Josh would be safe here for quite some time.

"Thanks for your help, Maddie."

She looked at him askance. "I had little choice. I can't stand when you get hysterical."

Kir gave her a wan smile. He'd been frantic after Josh mailed him Brad's name.

She hugged him tightly, then searched his face, her brown eyes a mirror to his own, though the rest of her was so different. They each resembled their fathers.

"I hope you find what you're looking for in trying to mend this guy, Kir. Be prepared for a less than rewarding experience. Zombies are easy to break and hard to fix. Good intentions guarantee nothing at all."

"I owe him this much. He saved me from Snow."

Maddie appeared ready to debate the point, but just said, "Ciao, baby." She punched Kir on the shoulder and let herself out into the early morning light. Mist rose off the small, nearby lake.

She had a long drive back to the pod. *The pod.* It was supposed to be a joke. As if all psis were the same when, in fact, they were all different in their own dysfunctional way.

Like psychotic Brad who liked forcing sex on normals until it killed them. Kir wished he had gotten to Josh sooner. They had moved quickly, in less than forty-eight hours, but Brad had done significant damage, what with a fully dressed Josh clinging to the edge of the bed, awake and rigid with fear, his eyes open and unseeing.

Some day Kir would kill Brad. It had to be done. He didn't care if the pod disagreed. It would be tricky, of course, but although Brad was stronger than Kir, Kir was a little more clever.

He heard Josh weeping. A desolate, aching noise. Brad would have used Josh's goodness against him, till there was nothing left of his original desires. Kir entered the bedroom to find Josh on his back, his shoulders shuddering in his sleep. No tears escaped.

"Josh," he whispered. Tentatively, he placed a hand on the moving shoulder and Josh flinched. Touch was going to be a problem and while it had always been an issue for Kir, it hurt to think Josh now carried that burden. Josh who had been so laid-back and comfortable with sex and skin and lovemaking.

"It's okay. You're safe," Kir murmured and Josh winced in his sleep. After Brad, words were too much like weapons and Kir hadn't a clue how to comfort Josh. He stared. Josh's freckles stood out in sharp contrast to his pale face. Worse was the tension riding Josh's body. It made Kir fear for him, though he refused to believe Josh was broken.

One of his few good childhood memories returned to him, his mother singing a lullaby. The words he didn't remember and words hurt Josh anyway. Kir hummed, no doubt off-key, and the noise didn't disturb Josh. After a while Josh seemed to calm, the weeping subsided and he slept, if not peacefully, at least quietly.

Kir went to prepare food. On their drive here, he'd bought plenty of supplies, leaving Maddie in the car to watch over a drugged Josh laid out on the back seat.

Today, if Josh woke, he would need light fare. Kir prepared vegetable soup. He'd bought crackers too, in case Josh was nauseated, and lots to drink because Zombies didn't remember to take care of themselves. While he cut up carrots, Kir caught himself fantasizing about setting up house with Josh and he had to knock the stupid fantasy away. Josh wasn't exactly here on his own cognizance and, the truth was, this sojourn was not likely to end well.

Kir knew that. He also knew he'd been right to remove Josh from Brad's clutches, even if it had meant putting Josh out.

It took a couple of hours for the drug to wear off and for Josh to wake. When Kir heard the bed creak, he checked the bedroom and found Josh facing the wall. His breathing had changed. Josh was pretending to sleep.

Though Kir wanted to speak, he decided it was wiser to wait until Josh was ready to admit he was awake. Quietly, Kir turned away. As he left the room, he heard movement.

He turned, ducking just as Josh threw, with surprising force, a rock. The weapon—a former doorstop had presumably migrated from the vicinity of the door to the bed—whipped past Kir's head, banged against the doorframe and dropped to the floor with a thud. Kir lifted his gaze from the rock to Josh who sat up, eyes blazing with hatred.

"Josh," said Kir and Josh flinched.

Kir closed his mouth. He needed to choose words with care, and he wasn't even sure what to say. He'd never been in this situation.

"I made you soup." Kir spoke rapidly. It sounded like an offering. Well, it was, though Josh shivered at his four words.

"*Soup?*" Josh repeated, incredulous, obviously expecting something dire from Kir.

"Let me bring you some."

Josh stared, baffled by Kir's intentions. Kir reached down and picked up the rock to take with him. Best keep it away from Josh for the time being.

As Kir ladled soup into a bowl, he heard Josh fall. When Kir returned to the room, Josh was on the floor struggling to rise. If only Kir could force Josh's panic away. But he wouldn't.

Kir spoke as calmly as possible. "You're too weak to attack me now, or to escape. Just take it slow. It's safe here."

"Shut the fuck up," Josh snarled up at him. "The sound of your voice makes me sick."

*Okay.* Kir wanted to help Josh back into bed, but it seemed best to leave the soup bowl on the dresser and retreat. Josh needed to pull himself together and Kir's presence wasn't helping.

Kir waited in the living room, though he wasn't sure what he waited for. Ten minutes later a pale, shaky Josh emerged, spotted the bathroom, used it, and returned to his bedroom, slamming the door behind him. All without looking at Kir.

♋ ♋ ♋

Josh didn't know when his life had slid into nightmare. At one point, he'd thought Kir had killed him and left him in some kind of limbo. But each time Josh woke, he became less surprised and more appalled to be alive. *To be kept.* By Kir for whom he'd harbored stupid feelings. He couldn't face it after Brad.

Josh woke weeping, with a terrible sense of loss. He was helpless to stop the tears. Brad had hollowed him out, then given him back to Kir. Or Kir had taken him. Josh couldn't tell. His will had been stolen and he didn't know how to think, let alone go forward. He searched for strength and found anger.

Night came and he welcomed the dark. He didn't want to be seen. If he couldn't be invisible, darkness was the next best thing. He welcomed the cabin's silence, too. While Kir slept, he couldn't tell Josh what to think, what to be.

He needed Kir to sleep forever. The only way to ensure such a state was to kill Kir, to kill his Minder before he took control. Took, as Brad had taken.

*Focus*, Josh told his brain. A brain that crapped out whenever he thought of Brad.

Josh required a weapon with which he could strike quickly and irrevocably. A knife or a piece of glass would slice through Kir's throat before the boy—the *monster* Josh had once hunted—could speak and bend Josh to his will.

Kir fed Josh to keep up his strength and he didn't want to think why, didn't want to think Kir had plans, like Brad's plans.

The kitchen would have a knife. Kir had sliced vegetables. The soup hadn't come out of a can.

Josh slid off the bed without letting it creak. He walked quietly. There were no city lights to guide him. The moon wasn't shining. In the dark he moved, taking care not to bump into anything. The crucial thing was not to rush.

Despite his painstaking efforts, a board creaked under his weight. He froze. From elsewhere, a bed's spring creaked in reply and, to Josh's horror, he heard Kir rise. Quick-footed and sure, Kir strode towards Josh. Kir was everything Josh wasn't—powerful, healthy, autonomous.

Kir flipped the switch and blinded Josh with light. He was caught in the kitchen and couldn't move. He could barely breathe.

"Hey." Kir's greeting disconcerted Josh. He squinted, confused by Kir's friendliness. Josh was bracing himself for an assault—he would fight, no matter the odds. But Kir didn't speak. He merely walked to the fridge to pull out juice and bread.

118

As if he thought Josh needed a snack. As if he knew Josh was terrified of Kir's words. Josh wanted to think these contradictions through, but he didn't have the luxury of time or clear-thinking—his trembling body betrayed him in a way he despised.

While Josh looked on, Kir put a sandwich together, all but ignoring Josh and his turmoil. Josh couldn't take his eyes off the knife Kir used to slice the bread. It was sharp, serrated, and Josh could use it against Kir's dusky throat. It wouldn't be the first time Josh had killed in such a way. He'd sliced open Snow's throat when Kir had ordered him to.

After Snow had attempted to rape Kir. *No, don't think of that. Don't think of anything but the knife.*

Kir offered Josh the sandwich. Did Minders feed their sacrifices? The boy's innocent goodwill freaked Josh out, so he didn't look directly at Kir as he passed the plate over. Josh watched the boy's steady hand place food down.

What Josh needed was the knife. He edged around the counter, leaned on it, then forced himself to look up.

Kir smiled briefly in encouragement and, oblivious, turned to wash his hands. *Now!* Josh's brain screamed. He threw his body forward, grabbed the knife and lunged at Kir's throat, his movements clumsy, but accurate.

The surprise on Kir's face was momentary. He shifted, arm snapping up to block Josh's thrust. Thrown off-balance, Josh stumbled back, keeping a death grip on the knife. Adrenaline shook him so hard, his teeth chattered. A second attempt now would fail even more spectacularly.

*Stupid.* He hadn't even cut Kir's arm. Josh was weak, confused. Panicked. He should have planned an attack, not taken the first poor opportunity. But there was no time and now it was over. Kir would speak and Josh would worship him as a god to love and protect. Terror seized him, coating his eyes with tears.

The boy remained silent, his dark gaze on Josh. At the very least, Kir should compel Josh to drop the knife. Instead, the knife remained in his hand while Josh vibrated with fear. It was an illusion, he told himself, that he had the power to hurt Kir.

And still Kir stood there, eyes black and fathomless, watching Josh like one would watch a wild, unpredictable animal.

Why didn't he speak? Disarm him? Josh's head ached and, transfixed by his confusion, he couldn't move.

Very slowly, so as not to startle, Kir approached him. Kir spoke no words, yet Josh was rooted to the spot and vulnerable. *Damaged.* He was damaged and Kir knew it. Kir gently extracted the knife from Josh's hand without touching him, for which Josh was pathetically grateful. After Kir backed away, Josh leaned down on the counter, dizzy, pulling in breaths.

"Why don't you sit and eat?" Kir said, as if Josh hadn't just tried to kill him.

Josh searched the words for compulsion. A useless exercise. A Zombie never recognized compulsion. He justified every thought forced upon him. For God's sakes, Josh had thought Brad was his boyfriend. Josh rested his head on the back of his hands, trying not to gag, appalled at his helplessness, waiting for Kir to say more. He couldn't understand why Kir wasn't talking all the time. He couldn't make sense of the quiet.

His brain was ruined, so Josh gave up thinking. He dragged a stool to the counter and, with trembling hands, fed himself. He made a mess of his sandwich, but he ate most of it. Kir politely looked elsewhere.

When he was done, they regarded each other. Kir appeared worried.

"I don't want your fucking concern." Unable to control his voice, Josh sounded histrionic. "I want to kill you."

"Um, yeah. I noticed."

"I really do." Josh whispered so his voice didn't quaver. He expected Kir to laugh. Fool, *fool. Don't engage in conversation. You'll lose.*

"You're exhausted," said Kir in his strange matter-of-fact way, as if Josh was recovering from a bad case of the flu. "You're better off if I cook for a few days before you kill me."

Josh laughed, though the laughter went wild. So little control and his shoulders shook. He wanted to weep again.

"I'm kinda hoping you'll change your mind by then," Kir added.

"*You* can change my mind any time you choose."

Kir crossed his arms and leaned back against the sink. "Listen to me. I am not going to manipulate you."

Josh's face arranged itself into a sneer. Otherwise he might fall apart. "I'll never know, will I?"

"You will know." Kir's quiet conviction scared Josh. "Your body will feel different. You won't get better if I'm working on you. So, I won't."

*Bullshit,* Josh wanted to scream, but he needed what remained of his dignity. Otherwise, he wouldn't keep himself together at all. He'd lie in bits and pieces all over the floor.

"I can't talk any more." Josh stumbled off to the bedroom.

♋ ♋ ♋

Though he didn't let down his guard over the next week, Kir was relieved Josh made no further attempts on his life. Maddie called a couple of times to check on Kir. He didn't share the rock and knife incidents. She wouldn't understand.

"He hasn't tried to hurt you?" she asked.

"Well, he's angry sometimes, and a little unpredictable," Kir prevaricated. "Mostly, he's worn out. He doesn't have much energy. I don't like to think about how much force Brad used."

She sighed. "Brad has admitted he got impatient. He meant to take his time."

Kir's gut twisted. "Fuck him."

"Well, we've given him an ultimatum, Kir. He'll be kicked out if he abuses another normal."

"Really? The pod actually admitted Brad is amoral?"

Maddie didn't like discussions about morals. "We think his actions were unacceptable."

"Unacceptable, huh? I guess that's a start. Brad mustn't like being given an ultimatum."

"Oh, he doesn't." They moved on to other topics while Kir paced outside the cabin. He had no intention of letting Josh overhear this conversation.

After the midnight sandwich incident, Josh wore a beaten-down expression. As if he had given up. Sometimes Kir had to urge him to eat and beyond that, Kir wasn't sure how to help.

Perhaps Josh believed he was Kir's Zombie. Josh cringed every time Kir spoke. He avoided Kir and spent most of his time in his bedroom.

And Josh slept a lot. Brad once told Kir he liked to push his Zombies as far away from their natural choices as possible. He also liked them fragile, eager and shaking.

*Oh, Josh.* All Kir could think to do was make Josh food and speak only when necessary. He hoped Josh's spirit could recover a little, even heal. After all, they had only been here a week. Recovery took time.

One morning, Josh changed his routine. Instead of retreating to his bedroom with his coffee after breakfast, he sat in the living room, mug in hand.

Kir tried to hide his enthusiasm for this new development. Sudden movements still startled Josh so Kir walked slowly over to the couch and sat opposite Josh. A coffee table lay between them.

"You didn't drink coffee two years ago." Josh's voice was even but strained. "I guess you still haven't developed a taste for it."

Kir shook his head. "It's not for me."

Josh nodded and Kir waited for him to say more. After a short pause, Josh said, "That was my attempt at small talk."

"Okay."

Josh settled back into the chair with his mug, though he looked far from comfortable. "I think you better tell me what's going on here. Not that I can make you do anything, of course. It's a request."

Thinking of what was best to say, Kir leaned forward and traced a fingertip through the thin layer of dust on the coffee table. "You want me to talk?" he asked, just to be clear.

"Not really. But the silence baffles me."

"If I wanted to control you by words, I could have by now. You know that."

Josh shrugged. "You can always change your mind."

"You're too fragile."

Josh's face heated up with shame. "Weak, eh?"

"Just the opposite. You're not easily manipulated, which is the problem. Brad had to work hard to get you where he wanted and it cost you."

Josh set down his cup and crossed his arms. He didn't speak for a while. When he did, his voice was tightly controlled. "Brad wasn't my first Minder. You were."

"I didn't make you this sick."

"Why not? You were desperate."

"I needed you to drive me to Atlanta."

"Ah." Josh wouldn't look at him now.

Kir chose his words with care. "I actually had a crush on you."

Josh snorted.

"You don't have to believe anything I say. But I brought you here because I owe you. You were good to me." *And I cared*, but Josh would resist that.

"Why would you think you owe me?"

"You saved me from Snow."

"So you wanted to save me from Brad. Kill Brad and we'll be even."

"I'd like to kill Brad," Kir said.

Josh turned sideways and used one arm to hide his face while he shuddered noiselessly. Kir looked down at the coffee table. He yearned to offer solace, but he could be no comfort to Josh now.

Within a few minutes, Josh regained control and spoke again. "What do you Minders do with your Zombies afterwards?"

"I don't have Zombies."

"You had me."

"No. *You* had *me*. And I didn't push that. You chose."

"I'll never know." Josh glared at Kir, trembling.

"I remember staring at you in the hotel room. You were sitting on the bed. I was in the chair, drinking wine, and you had just made it clear you didn't want me. At that point I toyed with the idea of pushing you, just a little. But I couldn't because..." Kir faltered.

"Please. Continue your lovely story."

"I just didn't."

"Why not? You wanted me to drive the next day more than you wanted sex?"

"I wanted you to want me." Kir met Josh's gaze and Josh quivered.

"I don't want you now," Josh declared, voice harsh.

"I know."

"The only reason I might believe this garbage is because I've reacted so differently. Three nights with you two years ago and I can walk away. Three nights with Brad and I'm an invalid."

"You wanted to help me escape, though you had reservations. But if someone wants to do what a Minder tells them, it goes easier. It's less of a strain. You wanted to kill Snow, too."

"I did? How convenient."

"He was an awful man, Josh."

"I'm sure." Josh's hands gripped the armrests, knuckles white. "What else did I want to do?"

"I don't know." Kir didn't know how to go forward with the conversation and Josh looked exhausted. Their silence was punctuated by the harsh cry of seagulls.

Josh's next words were obviously painful to him. "Should I assume that what Brad asked of me, I did not want?"

"You already know the answer. But, yes."

# Chapter Four

By the end of his second week at the cabin, Josh truly understood why those in thrall to a Minder were Zombies. He'd been sleepwalking, unable to think beyond his haze of confused panic, and only in the last couple of days did he feel relatively clear-headed. As if his mind was being returned to him.

Staying at this out-of-the-way cabin with Kir was not quite comfortable. And yet it could have felt much worse. Claustrophobic. Suffocating. Like a noose tightening, as Brad's hold had. Because Josh was living with a Minder.

It just didn't feel like it. Though maybe Kir had told Josh what to think. Brad had. Acid rose in Josh's throat as he remembered he'd thought Brad was hot.

*Don't.* Thoughts of Brad were debilitating. Thoughts of Kir were not.

Because Kir was here influencing him or because he didn't loathe Kir? Josh slumped and cradled his head in his hands.

This was the problem. He could not *know* if his thoughts were his own, or manufactured by Kir. All he could know was he felt better, more himself. Even if he spent most of his time alone in this bedroom he was beginning to think of as his.

He no longer wanted to kill Kir. The murder wasn't in Josh. Maybe Kir had taken it away after the pathetic knife attack, no matter that he swore up and down that he wouldn't push.

Josh raised his head and gazed out the window. Transparent glass. Blue sky. He had to look at things as clearly as possible. Physically, he was stronger. He could eat decent amounts of food and he wasn't sleeping all the time. He didn't constantly feel like he was going to crack up, only when his thoughts spiraled down into fear and shame.

He couldn't believe Kir was controlling him. Kir, who fed him and left him alone. The boy sometimes threw his dark, wary glances at Josh, as if searching. More disconcerting, each morning Kir's face seemed to brighten when he first caught sight of Josh. As if his very presence made Kir happy.

That couldn't be right. Josh was an unhappy, dysfunctional presence.

Josh's heart began to race. He feared Kir had planted an idea in his head. He could imagine Kir saying, *You can see I'm happy to be with you.* Though why so complicated? Kir could simply make Josh happy and be done with it.

*Stop!*

Josh turned and crawled into bed, overwhelmed by his brain's nonsense. He wanted a break. His mind agreed and he fell into a deep sleep.

Later that afternoon he woke with the absolute need to know whether or not he was in Kir's thrall. He had to somehow test Kir. It took Josh hours to make a plan.

The next day he wrote a long note and hid it under the bed. Last week, in an attempt to keep his head on straight, he had started writing notes to himself. Though it was entirely possible Kir knew, Josh couldn't remember Kir entering this bedroom after the first day. Not since Kir had hummed some strange tune when Josh was in his drugged half-sleep. A gesture that still baffled Josh.

He put it out of his mind and went back to writing, describing his plans to his future self. Josh was going to punch Kir, hard enough to hurt. If Kir had set up roadblocks to control Josh, to protect himself against Josh, the punch would never happen.

It was hardly a foolproof test, but Josh could not accept everything at face value. He didn't doubt that Kir was gentle with him, but was he in Kir's power?

Josh scrubbed his face. Why the fuck had Kir brought him here? That's what Josh could not understand. He feared he was easy prey. Brad had found him so. Josh shook at the thought.

He took two days to work up his courage for the act. During that time, he tried to be with Kir a little more often— enough that Josh would be able to throw his punch.

The test morning, as Josh thought of it, Kir made pancakes—he'd even whipped the egg whites. Josh found it hard to eat. His stomach hurt.

"More?" Kir lifted a fresh one out of the pan.

Josh shook his head.

"You need to eat, you know."

"So do you," Josh replied.

"I'll eat more after my run. One's enough for now."

"I'll eat more then, too," said Josh.

"Okay." Kir looked pleased at that. To date, Josh avoided Kir between meals and had yet to join him for his second breakfast.

After Kir cleaned up the kitchen, Josh walked onto the deck with him, to Kir's surprise.

"Where do you run?" asked Josh.

"There's a good path near the top of the road. I follow it for about five miles, then turn back." Kir was obviously trying to stay matter-of-fact, but curiosity shone out of his eyes. Josh hadn't done much small talk.

"Have fun." Josh stepped back. He wasn't ready to throw that punch yet. After the run. Kir accepted his dismissal and trotted down the stairs.

Josh was going to feel like shit if he managed to smash his fist into Kir's face.

Time passed and Josh stared out at the lake, dreading Kir's return and fearing the dread was of Kir's making. At least Josh no longer blanked out as he had with Brad. But he couldn't see his mental state as proof. Kir might be subtle. Josh sure as heck hadn't picked up that Kir had manipulated him two years ago when they were on the run.

During the next hour, Josh worked himself into quite a state. By the time Kir returned, walking back towards Josh, he felt relieved it would soon be over, one way or the other.

Kir looked up and saw him. Waved. Kir was in great shape, Josh noted. He'd filled out in the last two years. In fact, he no longer seemed like a boy, although Josh still thought of him that way at times.

In a fight, Kir would beat him, despite Josh's height advantage. Josh was weak and Kir was strong. Josh needed to find out just how great that discrepancy was.

Kir bounded up the steps and Josh's stomach swooped. He rose from the deck chair and, before he lost heart, strode over. Kir was breathing fairly hard and he placed both hands on his hips. His face was probably hot to touch.

Josh stepped closer and Kir went still. As if he didn't want to startle a skittish animal. Josh observed Kir's expression, open and sincere, but Josh couldn't let appearances stop him. *Act, don't think.* He tensed his arm, made a fist and threw his punch, all the while expecting some master move on the

Minder's part. Instead, just as Josh's fist connected, Kir's eyes widened with surprise.

Down the boy went. Josh stared dumbly as Kir fell to the deck. Josh waited for Kir to jump to his feet and, now that he'd been assaulted, tell Josh what to think. But Kir rolled onto his side, moaning in pain. Josh stared, amazed at what he had done and what it meant. He shook his right hand. His knuckles stung. In his anxiety, he'd hit harder than planned.

It was an odd feeling. For the first time in two weeks, Kir did not have the choice to speak and was incapable of controlling Josh with words. Josh should have felt relieved. If he moved quickly, he could tie Kir up and muzzle him, and thereby be safe.

But he'd seen Kir tied up and abused, and the idea revolted Josh. So he found himself kneeling beside Kir. The boy's eyelids fluttered and Josh reached for the pulse in Kir's throat.

Josh hesitated at the thought of contact, skin against skin. There'd been so little of it these past two years until Brad, when there'd been too much. But right now Kir couldn't move. Only Josh could touch Kir who, despite everything, was beautiful and always had been.

It struck Josh that he'd thought Kir beautiful before they'd met. Not like Brad who had touched and touched and touched Josh. Violated was the word.

Josh had always preferred control, well before his life had turned to shit. His fingers found Kir's throat. The skin was warm and sweaty, the pulse strong, and Josh was glad. He wanted to trust Kir, if the boy wasn't too angry with him. Kir might be playing some deep, convoluted or insane game Josh couldn't comprehend. Or Kir wasn't making Josh his Zombie.

Tentatively, it felt like a great luxury, Josh swept damp curls off Kir's forehead. The boy hadn't ducked the punch. He'd stood there, as if he had to take it. Well, Kir was no stranger to abuse. He had been Snow's punching bag, and more.

Kir rolled onto his back and his eyes opened. They were unfocused, dazed.

"I'm sorry," said Josh and the dark, unreadable eyes met his.

Josh couldn't help it, he flinched, fearing Kir would exact some kind of revenge. But Kir just blinked, waiting with terrible patience, as if Josh might hit him again.

Josh reached over and took a cushion off one of the chairs. He slid a hand under Kir's head and gently lifted it to place the cushion underneath. Then, taking advantage of the situation, he patted Kir's shoulder. Once Kir recovered, Josh would back off. But the boy lay still beside him and Josh found the contact easy. A strange type of reassurance.

"Sorry?" Kir asked blearily.

Josh sat back on his haunches. "It was a test."

Kir stared in incomprehension and Josh remembered how naive the boy had seemed two years ago.

"I'll get you some ice," Josh offered apologetically and rose.

He returned from the kitchen and placed a compress against Kir's temple. Kir took it, then gingerly sat up, watching Josh the whole time, as if Josh might attack again.

"That hurt," admitted Kir.

Josh nodded. "I wanted to know if I could punch you."

"You can," said Kir with feeling. "My head is killing me."

"Is primed the word you use?"

"Yes."

"I thought you had primed me so I would find it impossible to hurt you."

Kir's dark gaze bored through Josh. "I didn't."

"I know that now. But I couldn't ask you beforehand. You must see that." Kir didn't react. "I didn't *want* to punch you."

Kir winced. "Well, that's great to know."

"Of course, maybe things will change." Josh licked his lips. "I'm hoping you won't decide you have to work your magic on me now."

"Please," begged Kir. "Don't decide you have to test me every day or something, to see if I've primed you. I'm not fond of pain. I've told you, for all the good it has done, you're too fragile for me to work on."

"I'm better now. Not," Josh added, "that I want you to mess with me."

Kir shook his head. "You're not healed. You sleep a lot. You're too nervous."

Josh shivered. "Once I'm better you can manipulate me."

"No. I won't. Ever again."

They stared at each other and Josh was tempted to reach out to Kir, except he didn't want Kir reaching out to him.

"You're not angry that I hit you?" asked Josh.

Kir eyed him. "I've been hit before." He struggled to stand, using the chair for support. "I need to go inside. After that blow, the sun hurts my eyes." He swayed and Josh steadied him by the elbow. Kir looked up with interest, but all he said was, "Are you coming in?"

Josh followed. Only later did he realize that he'd stopped analyzing Kir's words, stopped searching for underlying directions. Not that he ever could detect the thoughts a Minder slipped into his head. But he no longer believed Kir was *his* Minder.

"Sit down," Josh instructed Kir and got them cold drinks, and Kir some ibuprofen from the bathroom. "I'm sorry," Josh repeated and Kir shrugged, eyes dark in his now-pale face. Guilt laced the relief that ran through Josh.

"Can I ask you a question?" Josh said.

"Sure."

"How long are we here for?" Josh feared this sojourn with Kir ending; he feared it going on forever.

"There's no time limit, though we need to get out before we're snowed in."

They had months. Josh gazed at Kir, striving to comprehend what the boy wanted of him, and Kir didn't look away. In other circumstances, this eye-lock might have been a mating dance.

"Why am I here?" Josh burst out, in something like despair. "I don't understand why I'm here."

"I told you. I owe you. You rescued me."

"Brad." Josh almost gagged on the name. "He agreed to *give me back to you*."

"He had no choice."

"Because your claim had precedence." Josh felt close to tears again. He couldn't cope with talk of Brad and yet he was forcing it.

"I just like you, Josh," Kir said wearily. "You were gentle and kind when no one had been kind for a very long time. I just..." He looked away, embarrassed. "When we made love, that meant something to me."

Josh's heart pounded and panic must have shown because Kir quickly added, "You must understand I don't expect anything from you. The cabin is simply a place to heal. It's a quiet place for me, too. I find it restful here."

But Josh couldn't leave it alone, despite the punch. "Two years ago, you forced me to run with you."

Kir nodded.

"And the sex?" Josh knew he'd asked the question already, knew Kir would give the same answer. Yet he needed to hear the avowal again.

Kir met his gaze and his liquid brown eyes pooled with feeling. "I was tempted, back then. I hadn't been attracted to someone who felt safe before. But the sex wasn't forced. You chose it."

♋ ♋ ♋

After the punch, something shifted in their relationship. Josh was more relaxed and, to his surprise, so was Kir. Josh had thought Kir would be jumpy and fear Josh turning violent. Instead Kir seemed pleased to spend more time with Josh, a reaction he found gratifying. He'd spent the last two years alone.

They went for short walks together to build up Josh's strength. They played cards—there was an old cribbage board under the broken TV. And they worked on small repairs. The cabin wasn't in the best shape.

"We need paint." Josh surveyed an outside wall. Bits of dirty white paint flaked off at his touch.

Kir scratched his cheek, as if he hadn't noticed the cabin's state of disrepair. "Okay. I'll get some when I'm next in town."

He'd been twice to stock up on supplies. The first time Josh had seriously considered escape, but had been too weak to make the attempt. The second time, he couldn't face leaving. He had nowhere to go. Now, he wanted to stay. Despite his initial terror, this cabin of Kir's had become Josh's safe place.

"We can scrape off the old paint first," he told Kir.

"Yeah?"

Josh smiled. "Have you never painted?"

Slightly abashed, Kir shook his head.

"You're a cook, but not a fixer-upper. Well, let's see what tools we have."

They stepped inside. Kir pulled the box off the shelf and opened it up. He stood there, fists on hips, surveying objects that were obviously odd and strange to him.

Kir glanced up, questions in his eyes. "Anything useful? Lots of rust, if nothing else."

Josh didn't look away and Kir blinked, uncertain.

They hadn't touched since the punch three days ago, although Josh had brushed past a couple of times and Kir had moved out of the way, unaware Josh made contact on purpose.

He still didn't want Kir to reach for him, but Josh couldn't resist lifting his hand towards Kir whose eyes widened. As if conducting an experiment, Josh carefully placed his palm on Kir's shoulder. The T-shirt was damp. Kir had jogged this morning.

Kir sucked in air but didn't move.

"A wire brush will do the trick," Josh informed him. "But we might want to buy a paint scraper."

"Okay, so..." Kir watched as Josh lifted his left hand and placed it on Kir's right shoulder. "Um, what are you doing?"

Josh slid his hands over Kir's shoulders and rubbed his upper arms, all the while breathing in Kir's distinctive scent. "You've been good to me, Kir. And I've given you little except a black eye. I wanted to say thank you."

136

Kir swallowed as Josh's hands came back to rest on his shoulders again. "You're welcome, I mean—"

Josh ran thumbs over Kir's collarbones. Kir vibrated under Josh's palms and Josh remembered Kir's past.

"Are you okay?" Josh didn't want his actions to be unwelcome.

"Yes, I'm okay. I just—" Kir broke eye contact, looking down.

"This isn't going anywhere." Yet Josh slid one hand against Kir's neck. "I'm not hurting you somehow, am I?"

"No," said Kir, fervent.

Josh laid a palm against Kir's cheek. "You're so beautiful. I just want to touch you."

Kir stood there while Josh stroked his face, tracing cheek and brow, even his eyes though so gently, before running his hands through Kir's thick, gorgeous hair, caressing Kir's scalp, his neck, the tendons that reached into his powerful shoulders. All the while Kir shivered and his arms hung at his sides.

Then it was too intense and Josh couldn't move forward to take the next step. Nor could he stay where they were with Kir relaxing into his touch. Josh leaned down, kissed Kir's forehead and stepped back.

Kir's eyes were wide open and dark, but not demanding.

"Sorry," said Josh.

"Don't be sorry," Kir whispered, his voice husky and appealing.

Abruptly, Josh crouched down to look through the tools. If he could have control, if Kir wouldn't mind ceding that to him, Josh thought they might become more than roommates. The idea made him dizzy. This intimacy was not to be rushed.

He stood and casually touched Kir's arm, as if they were buddies. Kir seemed overwhelmed.

"Here's what we need." Josh brandished the wire brush.

# Chapter Five

Josh told himself to wait at least a full day before touching Kir again. Josh feared ruining what was new and fragile between them. It wasn't exactly lust he felt, but a desire to touch, and affection. Feelings that had nothing to do with Brad.

Josh hadn't had much affection of late. At one point the agency had brought in some guy and that encounter had been lukewarm, given their sex had been a close cousin to prostitution. After that, Josh refused to have anything to do with the agency's "friends". Until Brad.

"What's wrong?" asked Kir. They were out for their morning walk.

"Nothing." Josh changed the subject, at least the one in his head. "Where will you go after the cabin?"

"I don't have plans."

"You'll probably go back to live with your sister and the other Minders?"

Kir lifted one shoulder. "It's not the best place for me. I find it hard to relax around them. I always wonder if they'll start playing."

"Playing?"

"That's what we call our magic when we use it among ourselves. I'm not a strong Minder, so I find others stressful. Except my sister. I trust her."

Josh swallowed. So much for changing the subject, because he had to ask, "Is Brad strong?"

"Yup. The fewer your morals, the stronger you can be." Kir picked his way through a swampy piece of path. It was heavily forested here. The air smelt of dampness and rotting wood.

"So you have all the morals, do you?" Josh was proud at how well he controlled his voice. No tremor and his tone was cynical.

"You don't sound impressed."

"I sometimes fear I only trust you because you told me to."

"I know," said Kir in a low voice. "I hope, with time, you'll believe otherwise."

"Does it matter?"

Kir shot him a look of, *you're kidding.* "I said *Brad* didn't have morals. We're not all the same, you know."

"Okay, sure. You're not Brad. Still, what do you want of me?"

Kir gave a short, embarrassed laugh. "Company, I guess."

"Hang out with your sister." Josh forgot to control his voice and anger came out. When he thought of Brad, the fear rolled through him, turning to rage. A helpless, weak kind of rage that he shouldn't take out on Kir.

After a pause, Kir said carefully, as if thinking how to word his reply, "Maddie comes with her own baggage. I don't agree with a lot of her, well, philosophies. You're easier company."

"So I'm easy."

"Don't twist my words. That's not what I mean."

They emerged from the shade and entered an open field. The ground was dry here, a contrast to the mud they'd trekked through. Suddenly, it was too hot in the still air, under the midday sun. The light turned harsh yellow, the air stifled, and Josh's rage shook him.

Kir watched him, now concerned. "Are you okay?"

Josh couldn't stop talking about Brad, when he didn't even want to think about the man. "Two years ago, you went with Brad, Kir."

Kir faced him squarely. "I went with Maddie."

"You took Brad's hand."

"To get him away from you. I knew how to handle him. You didn't."

"Brad touched your face," Josh continued. "And you let him. Why?"

Kir looked down.

"Because you're weak?"

Kir jerked his head up. "Maybe."

"Brad touched me all the time. I was weak," said Josh.

"Josh, you aren't psi. This has nothing to do with strength of character."

Josh stepped closer, he didn't know why, and Kir went still, not knowing what to expect, perhaps expecting a punch, perhaps expecting a caress. Josh pushed the boy's breastbone, forcing him back.

"You're a psi, a Minder." Josh shook. He hated the shaking. It came against his will and humiliated him.

"It's okay."

"*It's not okay.* You're hiding something."

"Oh, Josh," said Kir with some pain and Josh couldn't stand the pity. He pushed again and Kir stumbled as he backed up.

"Why do you take it?" demanded Josh, looming over him. "What if I decide to hit you again?"

Kir's gaze was steady, the bruise on his face fading. "I don't think you will."

"You're more certain than I am." With both hands Josh shoved Kir. "Tell me to stop. Use your words."

Kir, obviously at a loss, shook his head.

Josh raised his hand and Kir just stood there, watchful and wary. Unprotected. Waiting for Josh to strike him.

Disgusted with himself, Josh turned on his heel. Next thing, he'd be slapping Kir's face to see the boy's reaction. The boy wasn't Brad. They were both Minders, but Kir was *Kir.*

Josh marched back to the cabin. He could hear Kir, but didn't look back and Kir didn't catch up.

By the time Josh reached the cabin, he was sweating and exhausted. He walked straight into the bathroom and took a shower, hoping his overheated mind would improve under cool water. God knows it needed something. Every time he thought his Zombie fog had lifted, he did something stupid. Like hit Kir.

As if Kir couldn't have stopped the punch if he'd wanted.

After the shower, an ashamed Josh retreated to his bedroom, ignoring Kir who sat in the living room, probably reading a moldy book that had been in the cabin for decades.

Josh lay down on the bed until the worst of the anger faded and he felt more himself. He was grateful when exhaustion took him and he slept. When he later woke, he rose, took a deep breath and walked out to find Kir who looked up and set down his book.

"I'm sorry." Josh met Kir's gaze.

"It doesn't matter."

"It *matters*. I acted like an asshole."

"I mean," Kir amended, "I'm okay with it."

"Don't be okay with it, because it's not okay. Do you expect everybody to treat you like shit?"

Kir raised a hand. "Maybe we better not talk now."

Josh stalked over to him and Kir sat there. With some horror, Josh feared he would turn into a monster, abusing Kir who would take it, because Kir wanted to prove beyond a shadow of a doubt that he wasn't using his magic on Josh.

He sat on the couch and slowly, because Kir, despite his bravado, was uncertain, Josh brought his hands to Kir and cradled his face.

"I acted badly," Josh said. "You must call me on it." A tremor ran through Kir. Josh caressed Kir's face while his eyes darkened. "You must tell me if I shouldn't touch you. Because I'm telling you now I cannot handle you touching me."

Kir swallowed and Josh palmed his throat before sliding his hand around to stroke the back of Kir's neck.

"I don't know what you want," said Kir, an edge to his voice.

"I want you to lie down."

"*Lie down?*"

"I promise I won't hurt you. I'll stop when you ask."

Kir seemed frozen and Josh wasn't sure.

"You have to say you want me, Kir."

Kir shook his head and Josh pulled away.

"I don't think it's a good idea," pleaded Kir, as if Josh tempted him.

"For you?" asked Josh.

"For you."

"You're wrong. Do you want me to touch you?"

Kir looked away in a kind of despair.

"Unless I'm in worse shape than I thought, you do. Don't tell me that I can't read you at all."

Kir stared ahead, breathing hard. "I want to do the right thing," he said through clenched teeth.

Josh lifted Kir's hand off his knee and held it between his own. Josh's thumb circled Kir's palm and he shivered.

"I want to touch you," explained Josh. "I didn't want to touch Brad so reaching for you doesn't feel tainted."

"I just like you, Josh. I really do."

"I like you, too." Josh stood and pulled Kir to his feet. "Can I lead?"

"Yes."

Josh took them to Kir's bedroom and Kir looked up, eyes dark and wide. Trusting. Josh wished he was able to kiss but Brad's god-awful kisses were too recent. Instead, he laid a palm against Kir's cheek and the boy leaned into it, closing his eyes. Long eyelashes brushed Josh's thumb.

"Such strange beauty," Josh murmured. "You were beautiful before I met you."

Kir's lips parted but he didn't speak.

Josh's other hand slid down Kir's side. The boy, the *man*, vibrated under his touch. *Gentle, be gentle.*

"Why did you write me?" asked Josh. "Three months after we parted? Surely not because the agency wanted to find you."

Kir's eyes, unfocused, came back to gaze at Josh. "I missed you." There was a touch of defiance there. "And I wanted to make sure you were okay."

"I wasn't. I was the agency's prisoner. They hoped I could lure you in. But still, they were damned surprised when you responded to one of my many queries."

"I'm so sorry I got you involved."

"You didn't. The agency hired me, remember? You don't have to take on that responsibility. I should have known better than to sign on. But I was arrogant. I thought I could do the job. You proved me wrong." Josh's smile was faint and Kir looked uneasy.

"Would you sit on the bed?" At Josh's request, Kir gave the barest nod.

Josh brought his hand to rest on Kir's chest. Josh could feel the heart beating hard against his palm and he exerted slow pressure. Kir walked backwards till his legs hit the bed and he sat.

They watched each other silently as Josh caught the hem of Kir's shirt in both hands and pulled up. After a slight hesitation, Kir raised his arms and Josh took the shirt off. He pushed Kir back to lie on the bed and kneeled beside him.

Josh swept a palm over Kir's stomach and he quivered. "You've been working out," Josh observed. His hand moved upwards, tangled in Kir's chest hair and traced a circle around his dark nipple. Kir's arms lay by his side and he gripped the comforter beneath them.

"You can tell me to stop," Josh reminded him, as his fingers brushed over collarbone and shoulder. He didn't think he'd tire of caressing Kir's skin. Both hands encircled Kir's biceps, palms sliding up and down, enjoying the strength beneath them. Fingers trailed under the sensitive armpit and Kir sucked in air.

"There is so much to appreciate." Josh observed Kir's damp, tented shorts and smiled. He traced Kir's navel, then descended to undo his button and zipper.

Kir's cock sprung free and Josh captured it. His thumb circled the head, wet and deeply pink. Kir was hard and thick in Josh's hand.

Kir gasped. Josh looked at him, making sure. Yes, Kir's eyes were black with desire. Josh cupped Kir's balls and said, "You are so close, babe."

His hand slid up and down, one, two, three times. Kir made a guttural noise and arched as he spurted. Josh moved with him, carefully slowing down, watching Kir shudder in release, his eyes closed. Josh had forgotten how quick Kir was. Someday he would show Kir slow.

"Kir?" he asked.

Kir's eyes opened and, to Josh's horror, he saw tears. Fear gripped him. He had abused Kir; he was turning into a monster.

"No." Kir reached for Josh but, before contact, stopped. Kir's hand caressed air and dropped. "It's okay, it's okay. I've been celibate too long. I'm always too emotional. It's my nature."

"I thought you wanted it." Josh felt panicked. He couldn't stand their intimacy to be wrong.

"I *did* want it." Kir's voice was calm, deeper than usual and, unexpectedly, his mouth curved, a slight smile. Kir hardly ever smiled.

At a loss, Josh fell forward to rest his head on Kir's chest and listened to his heart whose beat was now slowing.

"It was good. It was right," said Kir. "I was only worried for you."

"Then I am going to have to worry for you," Josh muttered against Kir's skin.

"That would be nice." There was a warmth in the voice that Josh hadn't heard before and he relaxed.

He felt Kir lift his arm and Josh braced for the touch. It wouldn't be too bad. But Kir passed his palm over Josh's hair without really making contact. An echo of touch and somehow comforting.

♋ ♋ ♋

The next morning, Josh rose early, left his bed, and headed to the kitchen to make coffee. He was quiet, not wanting to wake Kir. After drinking one cup, Josh heard Kir's bed creak. Feet hit the floor and Josh's heart rate picked up speed.

A weight lifted off his chest when he saw Kir's face, for the boy's expression lightened at the sight of him. Josh's presence still made Kir happy. Josh had feared yesterday might have changed that.

Kir frowned. "Why so serious?"

"I was worried about you," Josh admitted. In a normal life, two years ago, Josh would have gone to his lover. But this was not normal and while he thought of Kir as his lover, they had only shared a hand job yesterday.

Kir shook his head, but looked pleased by the admission. "I told you I was happy."

"You did," Josh agreed, but his sense of right and wrong had been skewed by recent events and he needed reassurance.

Kir danced slightly and Josh laughed.

"Go, go." Josh waved.

Kir emerged from the washroom to see Josh in the kitchen. "You don't have to make me tea," Kir protested. "Sit down and rest."

"I can manage." At Josh's wry tone, Kir cocked his head so Josh elaborated. "See why I worry you just gave yourself to me? You are too obliging."

Kir's face heated.

"In a good way," Josh added. "That was a compliment, a nice thing, Kir. Don't let me take advantage of you." He had to remember that Kir's background was warped, that he expected criticism, not compliments.

Josh removed the tea bag from the cup. "Milk? Sugar?"

"No, thanks."

Josh walked back to the coffee table and set down the mug.

"You must know I'm attracted to you." Kir spoke in a rush, his face still hot.

Josh just smiled.

The rest of the morning was quiet, companionable, and Josh relaxed. He didn't touch Kir. Josh knew where touch would lead and he needed to build up his resources a little.

But in the afternoon, after he napped, he went outside to find Kir on the deck, trying to hammer together a rail that was falling off.

"Hi," said Kir as Josh came up beside him.

"You need another piece of wood," suggested Josh. "This one's rotting."

"I'll add that to my list." Leaning on the rail, Kir shook it. "Okay, not too steady."

Josh stepped behind Kir and placed his hands on Kir's shoulders to massage the boy's neck. Kir shivered and Josh stopped. "Do you want me to touch you?"

"I've been waiting," Kir said in a low voice.

"Good." Josh worked his way down Kir's back, massaging muscle. Kir's tension rose. Slipping hands under Kir's shirt, Josh stroked Kir's waist with his palms, back and forth, reassuring with gentleness, affection, care. All those things Josh had so missed.

"You can talk," murmured Josh. "Your words no longer scare me."

"Okay." Kir sounded short of breath. "But I don't know what to say."

Josh undid Kir's shorts and slid his hands to cup Kir's buttocks, up and down, up and down, approaching his crack, but not getting there. Not yet. They both needed more time. Pushing Kir's shorts down to his ankles, Josh ran palms along Kir's strong calves, enjoying the way Kir vibrated under his touch. Josh made his way back up to Kir's thighs, cupped his balls and Kir moaned. Taking Kir's cock in hand made Josh hot and he wanted to be closer.

He stood over Kir, his chest against Kir's back.

"I've never known anyone who smelled so good when they sweat." Josh kissed Kir's neck. He began his strokes and Kir gave an inarticulate response, something like, *oh* or *ah.* "What do you do?"

"Do?" asked Kir, in a bewildered half-gasp.

"And your voice is so sexy, did you know that?"

Kir shook his head, gave a sob of emotion and groaned, coming in Josh's hand. Grinning into Kir's neck, Josh licked the sweat. Kir breathed noisily, standing under Josh, trembling while his cock pumped and his cum ran through Josh's fingers. Then Josh remembered Kir had cried yesterday and turned Kir to face him.

Kir looked down. With his clean hand, Josh tipped up Kir's chin to search his face. Kir smiled his sweetest smile, the one that Josh, in his Zombie daze, had forgotten. It filled Josh with joy.

"Why wouldn't you look at me?" said Josh.

"All your compliments. I get embarrassed."

Josh laughed.

# Chapter Six

After three weeks at the cabin, Josh had asked Kir to lie down and, against his better judgment, he'd done exactly that. He wanted to take everything Josh could give him. Josh was the love of Kir's life though Kir kept quiet on that small point.

They didn't sleep together and Kir didn't touch Josh. At night, he retreated to his bedroom although he sometimes took Kir's face in his hands, a light caress, before stepping back and away.

Kir knew Brad would have kissed Josh a lot. Someday they would talk more about Brad, and Kir's history with Brad, but not yet. Kir feared Josh wouldn't understand. They were living in this bubble that had grown steadily more intimate and affectionate, and Kir couldn't bear the thought of breaking their connection. Josh liked to touch Kir all over before he came and Kir reveled in it. Every inch of his skin belonged to Josh. Sometimes Josh had an erection, but he wasn't yet ready to come. So Kir waited.

They began swimming. The lake had warmed up. Still thin, Josh no longer looked frail and haunted. In fact, he was the better swimmer of the two, though his endurance wasn't great.

After lunch, Josh picked up a book Kir had read. "*The Yearling.* Don't they shoot the deer?"

"Well, yeah."

Josh dropped the book on the coffee table, then plopped down on the couch. His hair, damp with lake water, made Kir hot. Well, everything about Josh made him hot.

"I hated that book," Josh declared.

Kir walked around the coffee table and sat on it, in front of Josh, their legs not quite touching. Kir watched for signs that Josh felt crowded. Instead, Josh's eyes darkened and he pressed his leg against Kir's.

Kir smiled to soften his words. "We should talk just a little." They never talked about much.

"About *The Yearling*? The boy is forced to kill his beloved pet deer, that's what I remember."

"Yeah," Kir admitted.

"I don't think I'll reread it."

"Josh."

"Okay, you don't want to talk about the deer."

"Maybe we could discuss the agency."

Josh went still. "Have you heard something? I know you have a cell phone and your sister calls for updates."

"Just to check on me. That's all. She has said nothing about the agency." Kir paused. "You must know they'll be looking for you. I've been thinking about how to protect you when winter comes and we have to leave here."

Josh's gray eyes simply watched Kir whose heart broke a little. Such a clear, kind soul. No one should have hurt Josh. Kir clasped his hands together so he wouldn't reach for Josh.

"It's only the middle of summer," said Josh finally. "Are you tired of me already?"

"*No.*" Never. "I just want to plan for the future." Kir took a deep breath. "See, I've stayed with the pod—that's what we call our little group of psis—because together we can make ourselves pretty much invisible."

Josh looked appalled. "Surely you're not suggesting that, come winter, I live with a bunch of Minders."

"No."

"Good."

"I want to explain that I've learned a few techniques from the pod over the past couple of years."

"Trade secrets." Josh had a strained jocular tone Kir didn't know how to interpret, so he kept his voice level and his delivery straightforward.

"Kind of. For example, when I was on my own, when you found me two years ago, my solitude was a red flag to people. The way I avoided everyone was conspicuous. Now I socialize a little. Just not too much."

Josh nodded.

"But I do something when I socialize." Kir realized he was wringing his hands and stopped.

"I can guess," Josh drawled, his face tightening.

"I prime people during casual conversation," Kir rushed out.

"Prime," Josh repeated.

"Nothing very strong or," Kir searched for words, "nothing to confuse them or go against their nature. Because confusion and resistance create their own problems. People become unpredictable. But if I slip in the fact that they won't remember what I look like, say, they usually don't care."

"You once told me that your sister primed Thompson. That he wanted you to escape."

"Thompson hated Snow, so my sister's directive would have appealed to him at some level."

"I see. And if it hadn't appealed?"

Kir shrugged. "Hard to know. Unpredictable." Josh's remote expression made Kir nervous. "I don't like pushing, so I just avoided people when I was on my own. But I could prime, minimally. To keep us safe."

"Us." Josh's eyes clouded.

Looking down, Kir placed his elbows on his knees and rested his forehead on his hands. He spoke to the floor. "It's just a suggestion."

"Because you want to keep me safe." Josh reverted to his voice from the first week, the one with no inflection. "What about you? What do you want?"

*You,* Kir longed to say, but the word lodged in his throat. Josh might not appreciate such a declaration. After all, Brad had wanted Josh, too.

Josh's fingers brushed against Kir's temple and he froze, as if movement would scare Josh away. His hand sank into Kir's hair and Kir leaned into the caress. Josh massaged his scalp. "Answer me, Kir."

"I want to be with you."

"Even though you don't touch me?"

"We're touching."

"Both you and I know it's uneven. Unfair."

*It will change.* But even if it didn't, Kir wanted this. "I'm in love with you." Josh tensed. Kir hadn't stated his feelings so baldly before, but surely Josh knew. Kir had tried to show love in so many ways. "If you don't want to be with me, I still want you to be safe."

Josh raised Kir up, all the while shaking his head. But there was a lightness to Josh's expression that made Kir's heart dance. "What am I going to do with you?"

Josh took Kir's hand, led him to the bedroom and, hands on shoulders, turned him away, his back to Josh's front.

"Actually," Josh murmured. "I can think of a few things to do with you."

Josh breathed in Kir's hair, kissed his nape.

"Josh," said Kir helplessly and was pulled closer so he could feel Josh's erection against the small of his back. A hand came up to caress Kir's face.

"Are you okay with that?"

"Okay with what?"

"I want to fuck you." Josh bit Kir lightly, where his shoulder met his neck. "I don't have to. I can just make you come."


Kir didn't answer right away and Josh couldn't tell if Kir was uncertain or speechless.

"I love you touching me," said Kir.

"Good." Josh slid a hand down to cup Kir's ass.

"There are condoms." Kir reached for the top dresser drawer and pulled it open in invitation.

"I knew that. I unpacked the bags after your last trip to town." As Josh wrapped a hand around Kir's cock, Kir grunted. Down came his shorts and Kir stepped out. Ankle, calf, the soft back of the knee—Josh stroked Kir's bare legs and the boy shivered.

"I'll take care of the condoms. I'll take care of everything." Enjoying Kir's trembling reaction, Josh trailed a tongue up the length of Kir's spine.

Josh explored Kir's balls and cock, but he was dripping and Josh didn't linger. He wanted Kir to go off while Josh was inside.

"Josh," demanded Kir as if he were ready now.

"Yeah?" drawled Josh. He loved this control, had always liked control. It made him hot, the way Kir clenched and unclenched his fists. "Have I told you there's a slow way to do things?"

"Slow? Now?" asked Kir in disbelief.

"Okay, later then," said Josh with a theatrical sigh. "Lean forward on the bed."

Kir obeyed and Josh palmed his ass, enjoying the hard muscle and the dark hair that dusted the skin. He slowly approached Kir's crack. He brushed the bottom of Kir's spine, not quite reaching his hole.

"Josh," Kir pleaded.

"You're perfect." Josh ripped open the plastic square and unrolled the condom down his length. He squirted lube into his hand and made himself harder. "Tell me what you like."

"Inside. Me. *Josh.*" The last word was almost a sob. The head of Josh's cock touched Kir's hole and his throat vibrated.

"Let's go slow," Josh murmured.

Kir's arms trembled as Josh opened him up. He played with Kir's balls, but it wasn't until Josh was fully in—God it felt so warm and tight, just right—that he clasped Kir's cock.

"Let's come together," said Josh. "Can you hold on?"

Kir moaned, collapsing onto his elbows.

"Kir?"

Kir shook his head.

"I'm close." Josh began to move. "Wait for me."

Kir pulled in breaths while Josh thrust inside and Kir held on, humming beneath him. Josh thrust harder, stronger, aiming for that perfect place.

"Josh. I can't. *Christ,*" Kir cried, coming, convulsing, clenching Josh. White heat spread through him—its warmth welcomed Josh back to lovemaking and he surrendered to the heat, letting go, inside Kir. Spurting, falling forward and a little in love, he had to admit, though not out loud. Not yet.

"Oh, babe." Josh shuddered.

He rested a cheek against Kir's shoulder who then collapsed into a boneless mass. Josh slid out.

He patted Kir's ass, then left to take care of the condom. Returning, Josh found Kir in the same position on the bed, unmoving and utterly relaxed. Josh smiled down as he sat at the bottom of the bed, on the corner so they weren't touching. Which felt wrong. And yet...

Kir pulled himself together and turned to look at Josh, flushed face, bedroom eyes, sated, yet thoughtful.

Josh didn't quite know what to say. Kir had declared his love and then, just like that, Josh had fucked him.

Rolling up to sit in a ball, Kir wrapped arms around his legs. He looked at Josh with longing and Josh felt bad. They should be touching. Josh cleared his throat.

Kir moved and Josh braced himself. His lover fell against him, to rest his shoulder on Josh's chest.

"Sorry." Kir moved a cheek against Josh's breastbone in apology.

"Don't be sorry." Slinging an arm around Kir, Josh pulled him close and kissed his hair. "You have awfully good instincts when it comes to what you should and shouldn't do with me."

"Um, I'm just following your lead."

"I always did lead. Truth to tell, it would sometimes get my relationships into trouble."

"I don't know how to lead," Kir admitted, sounding ashamed. Josh didn't know if Kir was talking about the entire relationship—in which case it wasn't true—or sex. They could explore that later, perhaps.

Josh hugged tighter. "Well then, we make a good pair."

# Chapter Seven

"Have a great visit with your sister." Despite Josh's attempt to sound sincere, his tone was hearty and fake. He desperately wished Maddie had never phoned.

Kir frowned. Josh could see that he hadn't masked his uneasiness.

"I'm just gone for the day," said Kir.

Maddie bothered Josh more than he could admit. He didn't like to think about Minders, only about Kir.

"Maddie isn't coming here," Kir repeated for the third time. "I'm seeing her in town."

"I know, I know. Don't mind me."

Kir regarded him gravely. "You're not going to doubt me now, are you?"

"No." Josh's attempted smile felt like a wince.

"The visit is bad timing, but I couldn't put her off. My sister is stubborn and it's better I meet her than she drive out here."

"True," allowed Josh. The problem was, he'd been living in a little fantasyland here, forgetting how Minders scared the shit out of him. "But why does she need to see you?"

"She can be overprotective." Kir looked away. "You see, when she left a month ago, she thought you might try to kill me."

"I *did* try to kill you."

"Fortunately you made a poor job of it."

"Don't joke. It's not funny." Josh felt sick to think of his attempts to hurt Kir.

"I know it's not funny, Josh. But it didn't count. You were still—"

"A Zombie."

"No. Confused."

"Okay, whatever," said Josh in some agitation. "But obviously I didn't kill you. You still answer the phone. Unless she thinks I'm impersonating you."

"She wants to see me in person and grill me. We can't talk safely on the phone. It's her way of showing affection," added Kir grudgingly.

"Okay, well go." Josh waved his arm and Kir just stood there. "What?"

"You and me, Josh, we're real, right? You believe that?" Kir's eyes were worried and deep with emotion. He lifted his hand towards Josh and stopped in midair. Josh reached out and brought Kir's hand to his face. Kir traced a thumb over Josh's cheekbone and Josh leaned into Kir's palm. The boy smiled, his eyes damp, and Josh turned to kiss the palm before moving away.

"Hurry up and leave, so you can get back," said Josh.

Kir moved away, running down the stairs and over to the car. Just before he ducked into the driver's seat he waved. Josh swallowed, but he waved back.

♋ ♋ ♋

Josh had forgotten a lot of things. Like what it was like to be loved. He wouldn't forget in half a day, even if he was nervous on his own. He was used to Kir's company. Dependent, though Kir never minded. Kir never minded anything.

No, that wasn't true. It was just that the relationship was young and they needed to discover each other, discover what lay beyond abuse and fear. There was always more to a person than their past, no matter how badly they'd been hurt.

Later in the morning, Josh dozed on the couch. He still slept more than normal, but the overwhelming exhaustion had faded.

He woke to the deck creaking and his heart leaped to think Kir had returned so soon. Josh stood, one foot moving towards the door before terror gripped him tight and he could barely breathe. Petrified. *God no, not again.* He couldn't endure it.

"Don't move, Josh." Brad grinned as he stepped into the cabin.

Josh should run, he should run. His brain screamed *run*, but he stood still, quivering like a fool. Hooked again. He didn't understand how this could be happening. Kir was supposed to be here, not Brad. Never Brad.

"Come to me, Josh. I've missed you. You missed me."

Josh *knew* it wasn't true, and yet one foot after another stepped closer to someone he'd known long, long ago.

"God you're already a mess, crying and shivering like a blubbering idiot. It's not very attractive," said Brad in disgust. Josh was ashamed and couldn't bring himself to look at Brad. "I followed Maddie this morning for this kind of greeting?"

The invader sighed. "Show me Kir's room."

Obediently, Josh turned away and led Brad to Kir's bedroom. Where he and Kir had made love. Josh didn't want Brad to know but Brad, smiling, found condoms and lube.

"I see that Kir is once again your Minder."

"No," denied Josh through his parched throat.

"Kir's a little more subtle than I am, that's all."

"No." Josh couldn't think of anything to say but that one word, *no*.

"You have to kill your Minder, Josh."

Josh sobbed, shook his head.

"You *must*. You can't be controlled by him any longer. Two years is more than you can take."

"I don't know how to kill," Josh lied.

"Nonsense. You killed Snow."

Josh covered his face with both hands. "No. Kir loves me."

"Holy fuck, he's really pulled one on you. Worse than me. I only made it lust. Look."

Josh couldn't.

"*Look.*"

Josh removed his hands from his face and stared into cold blue crystal.

"Look at what's in my hand." Brad spoke as if Josh were a simpleton.

He saw that Brad was offering a knife, handle first, the blade long and lean.

"Take my knife. It's my gift to you and you, in turn, must give it to your Minder, slide it into his heart. That's where it belongs. Do it during sex. The heart is where the knife belongs. Do you understand?"

Josh nodded.

"Repeat after me."

The words spoke themselves. "The heart is where the knife belongs."

"Good boy. I don't have much time. And you have caused me too much grief. Made me quite unpopular which, I can assure you, I don't like at all. Despite that, I leave you with this perfect gift. Isn't that generous of me?"

Josh nodded, a puppet on a string. Brad held out the knife, staring at Josh, and Josh's hand rose to meet the weapon.

*Kill your Minder.* The idea grew in Josh, became large with urgency, became the most important thing in his life. And yet, he could not open his clenched fist.

"Take the knife," Brad repeated. He gripped Josh's shoulder and Josh opened his hand, clasped the brown handle. "You're so easy to hook. Weak. But I like weak."

Josh's chest ached and he breathed as if badly winded. He didn't want to kill Kir, but he was weak and he wanted to kill his Minder.

The knife felt heavy in Josh's hand.

"Say thank you," instructed Brad.

"Thank you," said Josh dully.

"Give us one last kiss. Sadly, because the locals give such crap directions, I don't have time for more."

Josh lifted his face and opened his mouth. Brad descended and took control. His tongue invaded Josh's mouth and Josh couldn't think, he could only hold onto the knife for dear life.

The knife that belonged in his Minder's heart. Josh knew where Brad's heart lay. Brad grabbed a hunk of Josh's hair and jerked his head back to a painful angle. The muscles in Josh's arm bunched. Brad liked pain and Josh ignored his own. He aimed the blade. It sliced through skin and muscle, going under the ribs, slightly to the left, and up through the heart.

"Ugh." Brad's mouth fell away and his body folded in two, folded around the knife. Staggering back, he fought to stand. "What happened?" He stared at Josh, uncomprehending, dumbfounded.

"You're my Minder," Josh explained. "Not Kir." Never Kir.

Brad bent over gasping, blood running through his hands as he pulled out the knife and uselessly tried to staunch the flow. His gaze, blue ice, came back to Josh. "You must kill *Kir*." His words slurred, but they came out and hooked Josh with fear.

Josh went away then, he wasn't sure for how long, but when he came back Brad was on the floor. A puddle of blood seeped into the wood. The stench of the newly dead filled the air.

The knife lay beside Brad. Josh picked it off the floor, went to the sink and washed off the blood.

He could wait. He could imagine waiting and Kir would come home and they'd meet on the deck, Kir's face brightening at the sight of Josh. The knife attack in the kitchen that first night had been weak and stupid. This one would work because Kir trusted him. In fact, Josh could imagine Kir lying down and opening his heart to Josh's blade, submitting to the sacrifice because he loved Josh.

Josh gasped in pain, revolted by the vision. He dropped the knife and vomited.

*Clear, think clear,* he demanded of his foggy brain, *no matter what Brad has done to you.* He had to pull himself together. *Now.* He forced himself off his hands and knees and washed his face and hands, the cold water a welcome shock. He looked in the mirror and saw a wraith of his former self. Saw someone who could contemplate the murder of a loved one. A foul thing.

He had to run, fast and hard.

Returning to Brad's body, he searched the pockets and found car keys. After Brad's parting words, Josh could never trust himself again. He had been primed to kill a lover.

Josh raced up the road. At the top, Brad's car was parked. It started easily, the gas tank was full. Though he'd left the knife in the cabin, he was terrified he'd meet Kir on the way out, on this narrow gravel road, and attack him, attack his lover. When Josh reached the main road, he almost fainted in relief. Instead, he gripped the steering wheel and drove away from the town where Kir rendezvoused with Maddie.

After Brad's words, Josh and Kir could never meet again. Josh had to disappear where no one could ever find him, where he could not hurt the dark-eyed boy. Josh drove to escape.

*Minder*

# Dedication

To critique partners, past and present.

# Chapter One

The first time Trey Walters found him, Josh Mackay tried to put an ax through Trey's chest. He didn't quite succeed. The ensuing wrestling match lasted long enough to do damage on both sides. In the end, Trey's height and bulk forced Josh down, face in the dirt, knee to his back. Josh waited for Trey to break his arm. Instead Trey said, rather hoarsely, "I am not bringing you in."

It took months for Josh to believe that. By then the agency had not come after him and Trey had tracked him down again, bringing a few key items necessary for Josh's winter survival.

"How did you find me?"

Trey's smile was tight. "My special skill."

"What the fuck are you doing?" asked Josh when Trey threw down army rations and propane canisters for his stove.

"No sense you starving to death now."

"That's what *I* think. Why do you give a shit?" After all Trey, with Horton, had imprisoned Josh in the agency's compound for two very long years. He'd just recently been freed. By Kir. "Does your boss also approve of my new survivalist lifestyle?"

"Horton doesn't know." Trey dug out a few bags of coffee.

Josh's mouth ran dry. Months ago, right after he'd killed Brad, coffee had become a luxury he couldn't afford to carry with him.

"I didn't mention your lifestyle to Horton," Trey added. "Or to anyone else for that matter."

"Why not?"

"I have my own agenda." Trey was an agent, a good one, and Josh couldn't fathom why he was handing out coffee and food to someone the agency wanted brought in.

He scratched his jaw in confusion. "Yeah? That includes bribing me with coffee?"

"And what would I bribe you for? I'm just doing you a good turn. Guilt works in strange ways."

Josh didn't bother to hide his astonishment. Hard to believe stone-faced Trey felt guilty.

Trey waved away Josh's disbelief. "You haven't asked about your Minder boyfriend Kir."

Josh stilled, wondering if Trey would try to control him through his ex-lover.

"Can we make some coffee?" asked Trey.

"What about Kir?"

"The agency can't find him. Or his sister, or the rest of the psis. I thought you'd like to know he's free."

Josh hid his relief, though he didn't think he was fooling Trey.

"They found Brad though," said Trey.

Brad. Josh's dead Minder. Josh forced himself to meet Trey's gaze.

"You didn't tell me you killed Brad."

"No." Josh hadn't exactly been in a talking mood last time he'd seen Trey. Worry for his own survival had topped his list. Giving the agency information hadn't fit his plans.

"It took the agency a while to realize who Brad was. They think another Minder killed him. Internal power struggle is their theory. They suspect you're dead. However." Trey held up his hand. "You're not home free. They keep an eye out for you. Especially Horton who thinks you belong to him."

"How do you know I killed Brad?"

Trey turned his hand over, palm up, his kind of shrug. "Kir and you stayed at that cabin. Kir isn't much of a killer."

"Two and a half years ago, I was hired to bring Kir in *because* he was a killer."

Trey looked irritated. "No, because he was a Minder. You and I both know that Kir's a softy. *You* kill more easily."

Josh went cold at the thought. Brad's final vicious instructions to his then-Zombie Josh had been to kill Kir. Brad's words were potent. Nevertheless Josh had killed Brad and walked away from Kir.

Trey frowned. "Did I hit a nerve?"

"Why are you here?"

Trey walked over to the makeshift wooden table and picked up a cup.

"I was hoping for an explanation," said Josh.

"I am going to destroy the agency from within." Trey turned to Josh. "And you are going to help me."

Josh had to laugh. He was hiding out, avoiding the world, terrified the compulsion to murder his ex-lover would lead him back to Kir. "How the hell am I going to help you?"

"Just survive the winter. You've become a cause célèbre. Missing ex-marine, fought for his country, disappeared while in government custody. Some powerful people are very unhappy."

"No." Josh couldn't believe that. He had no connections.

Trey nodded. "It's true. At some point, when the agency is weak enough, your story can be the final nail in its coffin."

"I don't want to tell my story," Josh said through gritted teeth. Ex-marine, okay. Government custody he could deal with. Being Brad's mindless Zombie and fuckboy was not something he intended to make public. "I want to be left alone."

"Kir will be safer if the agency self-destructs," Trey pointed out. "But you have to appear at the right time. Now is not the right time."

*Kir*, thought Josh with an ache that never quite went away. He longed for Kir to be safe. From the agency. From himself.

The water boiled and Josh made the coffee. Trey left before Josh could get his head together to ask more questions.

♋ ♋ ♋

Josh made it through the winter. Trey's supplies helped but, truth was, Josh had Brad to thank for his survival. After Josh had knifed his Minder through the heart, he'd found Brad's car keys which had opened Brad's car and in that car had lain Brad's laptop with enough information for Josh to access Brad's money.

Josh had bought a canoe, winter camping gear, supplies. He'd dumped the car for fear they'd find Brad's body and trace the license. Two stolen cars and several hundred miles later, he'd arrived at the state park with his gear and gone as far into the interior as possible.

For someone whose thinking had not been the clearest last summer—being Brad's Zombie had messed badly with his head—Josh was surprised he'd done so well. The low point was breaking into the park's resort in January to stock up. He didn't enjoy his new role as thief and fugitive. This life was not a long-term solution, but he took a certain grim pride in staying free for nine months.

Josh wiped his brow. The snow had melted, the trees had buds and today he chopped wood in short sleeves. Spring had been a long time coming. He didn't know how he was going to survive the camping season with its swarms of people, but he was grateful the freezing weather had ended. He'd grown weary of fighting the cold.

His ax hit wood and the sound echoed around the lake. The noise didn't yet matter. The park opened in another couple of weeks, the tenth of May. Then park rangers and casual campers might notice Josh. They didn't belong to the agency trying to track him down, but they could report his odd presence to authorities.

If Trey already hadn't. During these last few weeks, Josh often thought of the agent, mostly because Trey had promised to return in April. Trey's interest made Josh suspicious, but he was also starved of companionship. So a couple of days later, when he observed Trey paddling across the lake, Josh's spirits actually lifted.

Trey was an attractive man. Large in every way, eyes an unusual light shade of blue, and a harsh expression that suited his chiseled good looks. In another time and place, Josh might have flirted with him. But not now, after Brad and Kir and the agency. Josh had found a certain peace of mind while spending his winter alone, but he was still not comfortable with company. And he missed Kir.

Dark-eyed, haunted Kir, who was too young and too old for Josh, who had rescued Josh from Brad and whom Josh was primed to kill. God knows that Josh, no matter how he loathed Brad's orders, had done everything Brad had ever asked of him. Including taking it up the ass.

Josh pinned his gaze on Trey, who was not a Minder or a rapist or a lover. Just a turncoat agent Josh didn't trust.

"Hi, Josh." Trey stepped onto the island.

Not used to talking, Josh simply nodded as he watched Trey tie up the canoe and lift his pack.

"Glad to see you're still in one piece." Trey looked him up and down. "You didn't starve."

"No." Last summer, Josh had been too thin, what with being the agency's prisoner and Brad's Zombie, but over the winter he'd worked to keep on weight. He tended towards skinny and couldn't afford it in the wilderness.

Josh swallowed. His voice was rusty. "So, how's the agency?"

Trey shrugged. "A little worse for wear. They haven't met with much success of late."

"They haven't found Kir?" Josh's pulse quickened as he waited for an answer.

Trey walked up the steep incline and his serious gaze met Josh's. "Not yet."

"Yet?"

Trey passed Josh and made his way to the wood table Josh had constructed so many months ago. Trey pointed at the Coleman stove. "I'd like some coffee. I brought some along in case you've run out."

Josh eyed Trey for a moment, then reached for the pot. He walked down to the lake, dipped the pot in the water and carried it back to the stove.

As Josh lit a match, Trey said, "The agency has sent Ed Harding in. He's made contact with Kir over the internet and I believe they've met once in person."

Josh didn't recognize the name, but inside he shook, fearing for Kir. He didn't think Kir could survive another intimate encounter with anyone in the agency.

Agent Trey would know agent Ed Harding. He was one of them. Josh, on the other hand, had been freelance, signing on almost three years ago for one apparently small job. He didn't know the personnel, apart from the few who had been his captors.

Trey waited until Josh set out the cups. Then he spoke in a flat tone that indicated he meant it. "Ed's a killer."

Josh pulled in a long breath and looked away.

"Ed looks like you."

"Fuck," said Josh in despair. Kir had a weak spot for Josh who, nine months ago, had left without a word. "Is he supposed to seduce Kir?"

"No, at least not sexually. After the story got out about Kir's mistreatment, as they named it—"

"Abuse. Rape."

"—the agency decided no agent should have sex with a Minder. For the agent's sake, also. I actually don't think it's in Ed to seduce another man. Though he has his own kind of charm."

Josh poured the boiling water into the two cups. His hands didn't shake, but he splashed some water on the ground. He passed Trey his coffee. "I don't have milk."

"I remember." Trey pulled out a packet of Coffee-mate, ripped it open and poured it into his plastic cup.

"Why are you telling me this?"

"So you can warn Kir off."

Josh turned abruptly away. "I can't."

"Can't? Or won't."

"I might kill Kir." Josh forced out the words. "Which is no better than Ed killing him."

He could feel Trey watching him. "Why would you kill him?"

Josh focused on the water, too blue under the bright spring sky. "Brad told me to."

Trey took a long drink from his cup. "You haven't done a very good job of killing Kir so far."

"Because I haven't seen him. I ran."

"You *might* kill Kir. Ed will. I promise you. He likes to execute freaks. His specialty."

For a moment, Josh couldn't move.

"You really care for this Kiran Brunner." Trey's softly spoken observation felt like a threat. People would use his feelings against him. Or against Kir. "One Minder you loved and one you loathed."

"They're not all the same," Josh rasped, finding his voice and barely keeping it under control. "They didn't all come out of the same mold. They just have a fucking gene in common."

"I don't think they're all the same, either." Trey spoke as if he had observed not all redheads were the same. "But the agency does."

"You are the agency."

Trey smiled, a rarity. "No. They think I am."

"I don't trust you," Josh muttered.

"I figured that out when you tried to slice open my chest last fall." Trey paused. "Look, if you don't want to do anything about Kir, I wash my hands of him. I just thought I'd tip you off."

"*You* tell Kir to steer clear of this Ed Harding."

Trey sipped his coffee. "He'll believe you, not me."

"I'll kill him, Trey."

Trey's face softened slightly. Unusual, but Josh hadn't been able to keep the anguish out of his voice. Trey cradled his cup in his hands. "Listen to me, Josh. You won't kill Kir now. These spells don't last nine months."

"You don't know that."

"These orders or primes or whatever don't last forever," Trey insisted.

Josh's mouth twisted in disgust. "I've done everything Brad Carlisle ever asked me to do."

"And more." Trey met Josh's defiant gaze. "You killed Brad."

"Yes." Josh flung his lukewarm coffee into the bushes. He'd lost the taste for it. This conversation made him feel restless. Trapped. Thinking about Brad did that.

"Do you think Kir would take advice from me?" demanded Trey.

Again, Josh stared out at the lake. Kir wouldn't let Trey get within speaking range. Trey had agent written all over him.

"Do you believe Ed Harding is a killer who has befriended Kir? Maybe you don't."

Josh jerked his head back to Trey. "I don't know what to think of you and your betrayal of the agency."

"The agency has betrayed itself and its purpose." The bitterness in Trey's voice arrested Josh's attention. "It only goes

177

after those freaks not strong enough to protect themselves. These are not the people most dangerous to society. We need some kind of police force for freaks, not a witch-hunt agency."

"Kir isn't a freak," Josh protested. Trey lifted an eyebrow, as if he didn't understand the risk to Kir of involving Josh. "If I try to get to Kir, the agency will nab us both."

"I'll help you."

"Why?" Josh's voice rang out across the lake. He could not understand Trey's offer.

"Because *I* am a freak."

Josh's blood ran cold. It had never occurred to him that an agent could be a Minder. Brad had managed to infiltrate an agency compound, but the process through which one became an agent was much more rigorous.

"I'm not a Minder," added Trey. "I'm not going to tell you what I am. Outside of this conversation, I'll deny I ever said such a thing. But my work is to undermine the agency. To protect my kind. There are innocents just trying to live their lives and raise their children. I will not let the agency institutionalize my people."

Josh looked around the camp that had been his home for nine long months. Well, he couldn't say no. If Trey had just laid a trap, Josh would pay the price. But he couldn't leave Kir to be killed by the agency.

"I'm just getting Kir away from Ed. Then I'm disappearing again," said Josh.

"Sure."

Josh rubbed his damp hands on his jeans. "I've forgotten what life is like outside this park."

"You'll remember. Your instincts were always good."

"What are you talking about?"

"Your file says your instincts were always good. That's one of the reasons you rose so quickly through the ranks in the marines. That's why you caught Horton's eye and he hired you to bring in Kir."

"This Minder business has messed with my instincts."

"I'm no Minder," said Trey.

"So you say. Yet you've convinced me to leave this park."

"Only because I speak the truth."

# Chapter Two

Kir glanced around Starbucks, feeling nervous. He shouldn't have met up with Ted again. If nothing else, the man was straight. But Kir found Ted's frank interest irresistible. They'd crossed paths on a couple of internet sites and, last month, Ted had been so enthusiastic about Kir's code that he'd given in. Kir had trusted Ted enough to meet in person. With precautions, because Kir recognized when he did something for the wrong reasons.

Ted's superficial resemblance to Josh lured Kir back for a second meeting. Like Josh, Ted loved his coffee. Between Ted's freckles, build and breezy confidence, Kir had been almost speechless the first time they met. Only when they sat down and Ted spoke—his voice deep and slightly mechanical, his face far less expressive—did Kir find he could think again.

They had stumbled through their first meeting, Ted oblivious to Kir's inner turmoil because Ted liked to control the conversation.

Josh had cared enough to let Kir talk. And Josh had been warmly attractive in a way Ted was not. But still, Ted lived nearby and Kir was lonely. So, a couple of weeks later, he agreed to discuss his latest debugging code in person, even though email exchanges were more effective and safer. Ted's one-track mind—and his focus on computers and codes—

convinced Kir he was safe. And if Ted was agency, then Kir would find out soon enough to disappear. He could even "ask" Ted about Josh's fate first.

Kir missed Josh, ached for him, though he couldn't confide *that* in anybody. He didn't know what had gone down in Maddie's cabin last summer, but when he returned from town that awful day, Josh had vanished and Brad lay in a pool of his own blood. In shock, Kir had hung around the lake—he couldn't stay inside the cabin with Brad's bloody body—praying for Josh's return. A week later Maddie showed up and dragged Kir off before the police came and charged him with murder.

But the police didn't arrive until a passing hiker noticed a funny smell coming from inside the cabin.

Kir often wished he'd waited longer, in case Josh had returned later, looking for him. But Josh wouldn't come back. Kir, like Brad, was a Minder who had forced Josh to his will. Though, unlike Brad, he'd never forced Josh to have sex.

"Kir? Are you home?" asked Ted.

Kir jolted back to the present—coffee with Ted—only to gaze into Ted's brown eyes and find them lacking. Josh's were the clearest gray Kir had ever seen.

Kir sighed. "Sorry."

"So, your solution is elegant and unorthodox, a fascinating combination."

It irritated Kir how Ted liked to lavish praise upon him. It didn't feel right.

"I haven't seen anything like it," Ted continued. "Did you bring your laptop along to show me?"

"I don't have a laptop," Kir lied. No one looked at his computer.

"You're kidding." For a moment Ted appeared distinctly disgruntled. Then his expression shifted back to amiable. "I don't suppose you could show me on your computer at home."

"I'll email you."

Ted was fishing for an invitation. Again. And Kir did not invite anyone back to his sister's. Too dangerous. He'd made a point to meet Ted far away from his actual home.

Today Ted was strangely on edge. Or at least Kir thought it strange. Perhaps Ted worked harder than Kir realized to exude relaxed charm. When Ted responded to Kir's frown with a big smile that didn't reach his eyes, all Kir's alarms went off. Ted might just be weird, or Kir may have missed the mark. He'd been sure Ted wasn't agency, but maybe Kir had become overconfident in his ability to peg the agent-type.

The idea made Kir sick, as all thoughts of the agency did. It wasn't safe to meet anyone, even casually. This paranoia was a burden, though a necessary one, and he had to acknowledge it. Kir felt a pang of regret. Not because he liked Ted. Only because Ted reminded him of Josh. Stupid.

He had to push Ted away, which Kir hated. It hurt his head and sapped him of energy. He loathed the glazed expression that came over people after he'd forced his words on them.

"You don't want to see my computer," Kir informed Ted, tone as bland as possible. It should have been easy to slip the idea in, but Ted reacted physically, stiffening.

As if he knew enough to resist. *Agent.* Kir kicked himself. A fucking agent and he should have fucking known. Who else would *want* to meet him? Kir's hands began to shake. He put them under the table where Ted wouldn't see them.

*Calm, calm.* He wanted to disengage without melting the man's brain, or getting his own blown out. Kir couldn't even manage a question about Josh because beneath Ted's disorientation lay terror. Kir could see it in the dilating pupils and blinking eyes. Ted had lost control. An agent's fear of Minders was a dangerous thing.

While Ted spaced out from the mild push he was fighting, Kir looked around the room to plan an escape route. Instead of escaping, Kir froze and his mind emptied of thought as he spotted someone staring intently at him from across the room, a *someone* resembling Josh.

*Couldn't be.* The recognition—real or not—felt like a body blow. Kir's chest tightened and he darted a glance at Ted, to see if he still sat opposite him, then back to the Josh-clone who shook his head in warning and disappeared behind a bookshelf.

Kir couldn't breathe. His eyes stung. Josh? After nine months?

"Kir?" asked Ted, coming out of his daze. He leaned forward, his expression confused and aggressive. "What the hell is going on?"

Kir rubbed his eyes. Josh wouldn't do this to him, play hide-and-seek in a Barnes and Noble. Josh didn't play games.

"Why do you look sick?" Ted eyed Kir, suspicion in his words and in the way his body leaned away from Kir.

"Sick?" Kir managed, worried he might cry. He needed to make Ted lose interest in him, not descend into hysterics.

After a long pause, during which Ted looked increasingly pissed off, Kir got control of himself.

"What the fuck is wrong with you, Kir?"

"I have to go," announced Kir. Josh-clone had warned him off Agent Ted.

"*No,*" Ted almost shouted.

Kir had to push, hard. He braced himself for the effort, focusing his mind.

"Keep your fucking mouth shut," Ted ordered. Kir heard a metallic click. "Open it again, you'll have a bullet through your stomach. Nasty wound. I know what you are, you little shit, and what you just did. Swear to God I will pull this if you so much as move those lips of yours."

*Shit.* This was idiot day for Kir. Pressing his lips together, he nodded to acknowledge Ted's threat and let Ted think *he* had the upper hand because, no doubt about it, Ted had panicked.

Kir's brain was scrambled, but he knew enough to offer no resistance. Ted wanted full control. Agents always did. *Submit, submit, until you can escape.*

"Hands on the table, Minder. I know your fucking tricks."

What bad timing on Kir's part, to hallucinate a Josh-clone. Kir didn't perform well under pressure. He'd fucked up.

Beads of sweat appeared on Ted's forehead. Kir might not have to endure another sojourn with the agency. With trigger-finger across from him, he might die.

Then Ted's eyes widened, as if surprised. To Kir's amazement, Ted fell forward, planting his face onto his half-eaten croissant. Blood trickled down his neck. What the fuck?

The guy at the neighboring table looked over in alarm and Kir said quickly, but with some force, "My friend is just tired. No worries."

With an expression of relief, the man went back to reading his newspaper. That he'd been inclined to stay out of things made Kir's prompt work without a problem.

*Move.* Shaking, Kir pushed away from the table and rose, resisting the urge to race out of the building and thus bring attention to himself.

Halfway through the bookstore, Josh stepped out from behind a bookcase and grabbed his arm. Kir jumped, smothering a cry of alarm.

"Shh. Keep walking." Josh dragged a numb Kir along. "I've got a car."

Under other circumstances, Kir would have been delighted by Josh's presence, his touch, his attention. Right now, Kir could barely keep it together.

They made their way out of the store and down the road, before Josh pushed Kir into the backseat of a car and climbed in after him. The car started up while Josh slammed the door shut and Kir looked into the driver's mirror and recognized an agent-type at the wheel.

*My God.* He turned to Josh in anguish.

"It's okay." This new automaton-Josh had no expression on his face or in his voice. "Trey's helping you. I promise."

*Agents didn't help. Josh, of all people, should know.*

"Where's Ed?" Trey glanced over his shoulder at Josh.

*Ed? Did Trey mean Ted?*

"In Starbucks. Dead," said Josh. "He pulled a gun on Kir."

"Where's *your* gun?" demanded Trey.

"I left it there."

"Jesus, that wasn't necessary."

"Yes. It was."

"What a waste," Trey muttered. Through the mirror, he turned his eyes on Kir, then asked Josh, "What's the matter with him?"

"He's in fucking shock." For the first time, Josh sounded emotional, angry in fact. "He's not a fucking agent, you know. He's not used to this shit."

"Ooo-kay," said Trey.

Josh's body was all muscle now, full of tension, yet in control, a hardness to him Kir didn't remember. There must have been something in Kir's expression, because Josh's face gentled. "I'm so sorry, babe."

Kir flushed with emotion—pleasure that Josh had called him babe and uncertainty because Josh's voice was filled with regret. They stared, and Kir couldn't reach for Josh because Josh didn't like to be touched anymore, not since Brad had harmed him.

"I can't stay." Josh's face, grim again, spoke even more strongly than his words. He didn't want to be with Kir.

"You're leaving now?" Kir supposed he sounded plaintive, but he hadn't yet wrapped his mind around Josh's presence, let alone his departure.

"Before Brad died," Josh said in a clipped, flat voice, "he primed me to kill you. I don't trust myself."

"You wouldn't kill me."

"I kill, Kir. As you've just witnessed."

"To save me. You would never kill me. Never." Kir had to believe that. He loved Josh as he loved no one else.

Josh jerked his arm in negation. "How the fuck do you know? You don't know what I am. You think I'm *nice*."

"You are." Kir didn't care if he sounded stupid or unsophisticated.

"Just because you let me fuck your ass doesn't mean I'm nice."

"For Christ's sakes, Josh, do you mind?" protested Trey from the front seat.

Josh ignored him. "Don't confuse sex and love, Kir."

"I know the difference," muttered Kir.

"I'm a killer."

"Let's not overstate the case here," said Trey. "You're pumped after the kill, but I know killers and you're not one."

"Shut the fuck up, Trey. I'm talking to Kir, not you."

Through the mirror, Trey looked at Kir. "Do your spells last nine months?"

Kir hesitated. "They can last longer. If the person is inclined."

"Josh, you don't seem inclined to me," observed Trey. "In fact, you seem downright protective. You don't even like me to call Kir a freak."

Freak. Well, that was accurate. That Josh had defended him made Kir feel warm inside.

Josh turned his gray, intense gaze on Kir. "I cannot be around you."

"Let Kir take the prime or whatever it is away," suggested Trey with some impatience. "Then you can stop fussing."

"*Fussing?*" repeated Josh, enraged.

At the same time, Kir said, "No." He looked into the pale eyes of this strange agent. "I don't push Josh. I haven't, for years. I promised. I *owe* him that."

"Make an exception so he can stay with you." Trey's voice was soft and persuasive.

Kir looked away.

"Can you override Brad?" Josh demanded.

"I don't want to, I don't need to." The idea terrified Kir. It had been okay to work his magic on Josh when he didn't know what Kir could do. But not now. Not after Josh trusted him. Kir felt tainted enough.

"Can you?" Josh repeated.

Liquid seeped out of Kir's eye and Josh looked away, swearing.

Kir scrubbed his face, hating his weakness. "Do you want me to push you?"

"Will it work?"

"It's not necessary."

Josh turned back to him. "*Will it work?*"

Kir nodded.

"Then for God's sakes take away Brad's last words."

They stared and Kir reached over. Josh hesitated for a moment, then gripped Kir's hand, his palm warm and rough. Kir never wanted to let go.

"You don't want to kill me, Josh." Kir forced the words, not too hard, but enough for Josh to feel it, for Josh to stay.

Josh's gaze became unfocused and Kir felt nauseated. Three pushes in an hour and this third one hurt. Josh's grip lessened, as if he wanted to retrieve his hand. Kir let go, feeling desolate.

Josh stared straight ahead. They hit the highway and sometime soon Kir should ask where they were going, but Kir could only think of Josh.

"I felt it. I should know. It's happened to me often enough." Josh turned and read the expression on Kir's face. "I asked you to, okay?"

*And now you don't want to touch me, because I've messed with you.*

"The prime is gone, right Kir?" Josh needed reassurance.

"Yes. If it was even there. You killed Ed today, not me. And you didn't kill me back at the cabin."

"I thought about it. I really did. Instead I threw up and drove Brad's car the hell out of there."

Kir nodded. At last, Josh had answered the question Kir had asked himself all winter. *Why had Josh left him?* But now what would happen? Josh looked so unhappy.

"Where are we going?" Kir, exhausted, felt dulled by events.

"A safe house," said Trey. Kir's eyes widened and Trey added, "*My* safe house. The agency doesn't know about it."

"Um, why are you helping us?"

Trey didn't answer and Kir looked to Josh.

Josh settled back into the corner of his seat, far away from Kir. "Trey's a freak, too. Or so he claims."

# Chapter Three

They parted company. In the middle of nowhere, Trey got out and disappeared into the forest. Then Josh drove for ten hours while Kir dozed. Josh feared he still had to guard himself against hurting Kir. The urge was no longer there, but the image he'd found in his mind so many months ago, that of spearing Kir's heart with Brad's long knife, haunted him.

It was *only* an image. Planted by Brad. Josh had chosen not to act. As if repeating these facts made Kir safer. No, Kir was safe because he had forced Brad's words away from Josh, leaving him rattled and Kir exhausted.

They entered the city at midnight and deep within some unexceptional subdivision, Josh drove into the driveway of a rather upscale townhouse. He thumbed the garage-door opener and Kir woke.

Josh stared straight ahead, pulling into the too-bright garage. He closed the garage door behind them.

He turned to Kir. "I've never been here before. I don't know that Trey is trustworthy, but after Ed's little performance, I can tell you Trey didn't lie when he said you were in danger."

Kir blinked at him.

"Kir?" asked Josh.

"Let's go inside then." Kir, not quite awake, had gravel in his voice. Josh had not forgotten how sexy Kir's voice was, deep and rich, but now was not the time to remember.

Josh left the car and Kir followed. They didn't have much to carry, just Josh's bag. According to Trey, the townhouse had supplies. Josh hoped it was true.

He rifled through the kitchen and found lots to drink. Boxed juice, bottled water. As Josh poured himself some water, Kir opened the freezer.

He turned to Josh. "I'm hungry. Should I throw in one of these frozen pizzas?"

Noise roared through his head. Josh stiffened in fear, aware of the glass in his hand only after it broke, cutting his palm. Beyond that, he couldn't think.

When the noise subsided, Kir was beside him, trying to open Josh's wet fist while Josh clung to the pain.

"Josh. Please let go."

He breathed in once, then slowly unclenched his fist. The blood ran. Kir's hands shook, but he took out the large shard that had sliced Josh's palm. He led Josh to the sink to run water over the injured hand. The cold water soothed. The noise in Josh's head receded.

"It's not a deep cut." Josh kept his voice even. "I was lucky. Check the bathroom for a first-aid kit."

Kir eyed him and Josh nodded encouragement. "I'll be okay while you get a first-aid kit. I'll bet Trey has stocked this place well. Just look at the kitchen."

"Okay." Kir dashed away while Josh let the cold water numb his hand. He just focused on that numbness. He needed it.

Kir was back, touching him, soothing Josh's frayed nerves with his careful attention. Kir dried the hand with a clean cloth, applied antibiotic cream, then gauze and tape. Loosely clasping Josh's wrist, he drew Josh to a kitchen chair and pressed lightly on Josh's shoulder until he sat.

The rules had changed. Last summer, only Josh could touch Kir. Josh's body had been sensitized by his time as Brad's Zombie. Josh shuddered at the memory and Kir, misreading Josh's body language, backed off.

"No," said Josh. "I'm just remembering too much. Always a mistake. Brad ate a lot of frozen pizza."

"I'm sorry. I should have known. My brain's slow today."

"I can't eat frozen pizza, that's all."

Kir reached for Josh again, then checked himself. But unlike last summer, Josh, while not exactly the most relaxed he'd ever been, wanted that contact.

"Come here." He opened his arms.

Kir looked at a loss at the change of rules, so Josh stood and pulled Kir into a hug, a little roughly as he remembered Ed and that fucking gun. He wanted Kir safe.

"Goddammit," Josh swore into Kir's hair because he felt too much and he couldn't explain anything. Kir grabbed him, clutching his back, trembling. Though no calmer than Kir, Josh made shushing noises. There was solace in their embrace. Josh ran a hand through Kir's thick, tangled hair to calm Kir, to calm himself. Kir's tears dampened Josh's neck. He didn't know how long they stood like that but, eventually, they came to rest their foreheads against each other.

"Despite my PTSD"—Josh had never wanted PTSD, well who did, but now he had it in spades—"we need to eat and drink."

"There's some kind of lasagna in there."

"Perfect." Josh stepped back before he started kissing Kir. If they made out now, they would never got their meal and Kir needed to eat.

Kir retrieved a frozen tray of food from the freezer and stuck it in the oven. He poured them both juice and ripped open a bag of popcorn. "Let's sit in a room with more comfortable chairs."

A couch and a coffee table made up the living room. They settled there, Kir stuffing his face while Josh could barely swallow. Though he forced himself to drink, his appetite was shot. Stress did that. Kir noticed and Josh just shook his head.

"Give me time. I'll be able to eat later."

"I'll get you another drink." Kir went back to the kitchen and Josh could hear him cleaning up the glass he'd dropped earlier. Kir, endlessly thoughtful, incredibly kind. Josh embarrassed himself by blinking back tears as he remembered how Kir had cared for him during his first days after Brad, when Josh had been a physical and emotional wreck, and Kir hadn't flinched from Josh's attempts to hurt him.

Kir returned to the living room and Josh held out a hand. Kir took it without hesitation. Josh drew him into his lap. Kir curled into him.

Josh's cock went hard against Kir's butt.

Kir met his gaze. "I thought you hated me."

"No." Josh palmed Kir's cheek, then carefully touched Kir's eyes, his brow, his temples, his wide mouth, remembering the beauty there, because Kir was, by any standard, gorgeous. He submitted to Josh's touch, as he always did, eyes darkening with desire.

"I'm not going to hurt you," said Josh.

Kir frowned. "I know that."

"I didn't. I was terrified I'd kill you."

"You wouldn't."

"Such belief."

"Yes."

Josh cradled Kir's face in his hands. "I missed you all winter."

Solemn, Kir gazed back, unable or unwilling to respond. With his thumb, Josh traced Kir's lips.

"I didn't forget how beautiful you are."

Kir's lips parted.

"Do you mind being called beautiful? Some guys don't like it. I could say you're hot and it would be true, but you're beautifully hot."

Kir blushed and Josh leaned forward to press his lips against Kir's. Kir stilled, perhaps because of his own personal demons, perhaps fear for Josh. He tongued Kir's lips. Kir groaned, opened his mouth, and Josh plundered. Kir's mouth was sweet with juice, salty with popcorn, all Kir-taste and eagerness. The kiss took over and soon they were grappling with each other, making out for all they were worth, making up for their lost year.

They kneeled on the couch, chest to chest, hard cocks pressed against each other, unable to get close enough despite deep kisses tinged with desperation. Josh broke away and yanked off Kir's shirt while Kir unzipped Josh's jeans.

Then Josh's cock was deep in Kir's mouth. Kir massaged his balls. Josh couldn't pull in enough air as he rested his hands on Kir's warm back. Kir rose and fell. Josh's cock pushed deeper with each stroke, feeling the warmth and the tongue and the back of the throat, unable to think beyond sensation. After a time he began to shake with lust and emotion, caught on the edge of a precipice.

"Kir," he warned as he stiffened. But Kir kept the rhythm going and Josh stopped fighting the release. He let go, spurting.

Despite that, Kir didn't stop his attentions. He thoroughly licked Josh's head and slit, even after it was slack with gratitude. Josh caressed Kir's back, feather touches with his rough fingers because he remembered that his lover, above all else, wanted contact.

Kir looked up, dazed, and yet the uncertainty that always cut Josh lurked in his eyes. As if he thought Josh might criticize him.

"Hi, gorgeous." Josh leaned forward and kissed Kir, tasting himself in Kir's mouth.

Kir responded with eagerness, clutching Josh's shoulders, shivering in his embrace.

During their short times together, there had been little opportunity to kiss and Josh couldn't predict their future. While they kissed, Josh took his time undressing Kir, making away with his pants. Without disengaging, he arranged Kir to sit on his lap facing him, Josh's cock still sated and Kir's rock hard.

Liquid seeped out Kir's slit and Josh circled the head with his fingers. Kir's chest rumbled with heat and Josh pulled Kir closer, tipping up his ass, one hand with Kir's cock, the other holding Kir's balls.

Josh broke the kiss to look at Kir, whose lips were swollen with kissing, whose face was heated with pleasure.

"Hey, babe," said Josh and his fingers slowly moved back from Kir's balls.

"Josh."

"Yes?" Josh reached the edge of Kir's hole and Kir's gaze became unfocused. Josh's middle finger, slick with Kir's precum, made contact and Kir opened for him. He slid in his finger and Kir almost fell backwards.

Josh left Kir's cock to catch him. They shifted so Kir's knees were on either side of Josh's thighs and Kir could lean on Josh, breathing noisily, Josh's finger up Kir's ass, relaxing him and massaging him. He brought a second finger inside and Kir moaned.

The oven bell dinged and Kir stiffened, distracted.

"Don't think about leaving me now," Josh warned. Kir was so close. Josh used his free hand to pump Kir. Once, twice, and the third time, Kir's white cum spilled across Josh's fist and onto his thigh while Kir shuddered above him.

He didn't remove his fingers right away. Instead he kissed Kir as deeply as he could and Kir took everything Josh could give.

Josh slid out, tamped down the kiss and let Kir go. With a bewildered air, Kir backed off the couch and walked naked to the kitchen. Josh washed his hands, changing the bandage. His cut had bled during their speed sex, but not a lot.

They ate hungrily now, not speaking, and when they finished, Josh's exhaustion threatened to overtake him.

Kir noticed. "Bed for you."

They went upstairs and found the master bedroom with a queen-sized bed. Kir lingered near the doorway, uncertain what to do, and Josh remembered that last summer he'd refused to sleep in the same bed as Kir.

"You," he told Kir, "are with me." He took Kir's hand and they tumbled into bed. "Tomorrow, we have a lot to talk about. Should have been tonight, but, well, you know."

Sleep about to claim him, Josh pulled Kir's back against his chest and Kir moved closer, kissing Josh's arm.

As he slipped away, he heard Kir whisper, "I love you."

♋ ♋ ♋

Early morning, before the sun rose, Josh woke disoriented. No longer in his one-man tent, he'd somehow ended up naked in a luxurious bed. He felt safe, if confused. Then his heart stuttered awake to see why. He'd slept with Kir, his beloved. Josh had named him thus last winter, though he couldn't yet say it aloud.

When they'd fallen asleep, Kir had been relaxed, but now there was tension in his back and he was curled up on the other side of the bed. With a pang, Josh wondered when Kir had slept with someone he wanted to be with. Apart from Josh that one time.

Josh rolled out of bed and explored the washroom. Yes, Trey had supplies. Josh opened the box of condoms and while there wasn't lube, there was oil.

He turned off the bathroom light and padded back into the bedroom, letting his eyes adjust to the gray darkness, listening to Kir breathe. Kir jumped in his sleep. If Kir had been sleeping peacefully, Josh would have let him be.

He placed the oil and condom on the side table and climbed back into bed, crawling over to Kir's side and looking down at him. He wanted to protect Kir from his past, an impossibility. They could only move forward.

He laid his hand on Kir's shoulder, very little pressure, and Kir jerked awake.

"Hey," Josh murmured. "It's okay."

"Josh?" Kir tried to turn, but Josh kept pressure on his shoulder.

"Lie on your stomach. Look away from me."

"Um, okay." Kir sounded confused, unsure. He paused for a moment, then rested his head on the back of his hands, facing away. Josh could feel the tension in his body. During their few weeks together last summer, they'd made love frequently. Too often, when foreplay began, Kir had been overanxious to please and only relaxed when Josh gave orders. Josh didn't know if Kir had simply been worried about Josh and his sensitivity to touch, or if making love—at least its opening movements—stressed Kir.

Josh leaned over Kir, brushed his hair back from his face and kissed the salty corner of Kir's eye.

"Dreaming?" Josh asked.

"I guess."

"Bad dream?"

"I don't remember."

Josh stroked Kir's upper arm and kissed his cheek. "You've been working out. Your muscles make me hot." He kissed the corner of Kir's mouth. "As does your mouth. Well, everything about you."

Kir snorted in surprise. He always reacted to compliments as if they were embarrassing bolts out of the blue.

"You know I like everything about you, right?"

Kir's lips parted. "I'm glad," he declared with such feeling that Josh's chest squeezed tight.

"Did you know?"

Kir gave a short shake of his head.

"Do you want me to touch you?" asked Josh.

"*Yes.*"

"Good, because I've been dying to touch you for months. It hurt to think of you." Josh bit Kir's neck lightly and Kir gasped. "Did you ever think of me?"

"All the time."

Josh smiled. He stroked under Kir's arm while he licked the skin he'd nipped. "You taste like salt and Kir. Perfect. I remembered your taste, you know. I dreamed of it sometimes."

A tear leaked out of Kir's eye. He had always been emotional, as Josh had learned during their weeks together. He came back to catch the salty tear on his tongue, then laved Kir's eye shut.

"You worry too much, just when you're not supposed to," said Josh.

"I'm sorry."

"I don't want you to be sorry. I want you to want me."

"I want you, Josh."

"I want to fuck you. Okay?"

"Yes."

"You should check that I have condoms. God knows what Brad carried around with him."

"I know you have condoms."

Josh laughed, stroking Kir's back, the shoulder blades, the muscles beneath skin, the dusting of dark hair. "You're right, but you didn't know. You just like to say yes, because I'm going to fuck your brains out."

Kir raised his ass in invitation. Josh palmed Kir's cheeks appreciatively, then stroked his legs before spreading them farther apart. "Stay like that, okay?"

"Okay," said Kir thickly.

Josh smiled. "I love your voice."

"My voice?"

"So sexy."

Kir didn't answer. Josh reached under to find Kir's cock hard and dripping.

"Have you slowed down any?" asked Josh.

"I don't know." Kir sounded bewildered by all this talk. He always came quickly, at least with Josh, and Josh didn't know if that was a personal quirk or anxiety or youth. Though Kir, no longer the boy of twenty-two he'd first met, was twenty-five to Josh's thirty-one.

"If you don't know, Kir, who does?" Josh held Kir's cock, gently squeezing it, running his fingertips over Kir's slick head. Kir became even harder.

"You," Kir managed.

"Remember sometimes we'd come together?"

Kir rested on his elbows now. "I don't know if I can wait, Josh," he pleaded.

"What do you want?"

Kir didn't answer, though he was noisily inarticulate as Josh stroked Kir's length in a rhythm that would bring release.

"I'll tell you what I want," said Josh and Kir groaned. "Exactly that." Kir came, pumping into Josh's hand, shuddering while Josh palmed Kir's back with his clean hand.

"At least, that's what I wanted first. Now, don't move." Josh collected Kir's cum. Kir stayed still, shivering a little, ass raised, elbows braced, pleasure noises coming from his throat. Josh couldn't remember anyone enjoying his attentions as much as Kir did.

Josh slathered Kir's cum up and down Kir's crack, then reached for the condom and rolled it up his length.

"Are you relaxed?" Josh touched the tip of his cock to Kir's perfect hole.

"Please."

"Oh, I want it, babe, you don't have to ask." Josh pushed in and Kir welcomed him, muscles relaxing to take him, throat humming, yes.

"You amaze me, Kir. You just let me in. No resistance. As if we belong together."

Josh rested there, savoring the heat and the feel of Kir, filling Kir to the hilt.

"Are you comfortable?"

"*Josh.*" Not an answer, but it sounded good.

Instead of moving, Josh stroked Kir's legs and lightly touched his balls and the seam down their middle.

"Josh." Not a plea, just a statement.

"I'm here. I'm not going anywhere."

Kir repeated his name. Josh began to move. He started slow. He wanted to feel everything about it, the way Kir's muscles clenched and released, the way Kir's legs trembled. He wanted to listen to Kir moan. But at some point all these observations fell by the wayside and Josh's control lost the upper hand. He thrust harder and harder. His cock took over. There was sensation and Kir and motion and emotion till the wave hit him and he released, panting above Kir who still hadn't moved, yet his entire body vibrated with pleasure. Josh did not want to leave.

His penis didn't soften right away so instead of slipping out, he slung an arm under Kir's stomach and sat back, bringing Kir with him. As if to end things as they had begun, he bit Kir's neck again and Kir didn't even gasp, he just rested, boneless in Josh's arms.

Josh nuzzled Kir. "No more bad dreams tonight, okay?"

"Okay."

They tumbled over, Josh slid out and Kir turned. They lay side by side, facing each other, and kissed long and deep and slow before they fell asleep.

# Chapter Four

Kir woke enveloped in Josh's warmth, his shoulder absorbing the heat from Josh's chest. Their legs intertwined, Kir lay on his back, when he only ever slept curled on his side. Then again, he was sleeping with Josh. Kir opened his eyes tentatively, as if Josh might disappear in the bright light of day. Instead, clear gray eyes looked down at him. With affection, thought Kir, and like a school girl his heart leapt with delight.

"Good morning," greeted Josh, a slight question in his voice, needing reassurance. Because Josh worried about Kir and his past and his reaction to sex.

Kir turned and ducked his head into Josh's neck so he wouldn't look too love struck.

"Yes," he declared, feeling ardent.

Josh stroked Kir's back and Kir felt the bandage on Josh's palm.

With alarm, Kir sat up. He grabbed Josh's hand. "How is the cut?"

Josh smiled as Kir examined him. "It's fine. I changed the bandage a couple of times. I was perhaps a little too active."

"I'm sorry." Kir traced the skin around the bandage and Josh shivered.

"Not your fault." Josh could say that because he didn't yet know Brad had come after him because of Kir.

"It is," Kir said in a low voice.

Josh's bandaged hand rose, nudging Kir's chin up so he had to meet Josh's gaze. "What is your fault? That I cut myself?"

"Brad." Kir almost gagged on the name.

Josh's mouth twisted and his gray eyes clouded. "Why bring Brad into our bed?"

Kir could barely breathe now.

Josh sighed. "Why do you feel responsible for Brad's actions? Because he was a fellow Minder?"

"No." Kir closed his eyes, ashamed. Josh, at least, had been Brad's Zombie.

The silence stretched on and Kir knew he had to speak. He'd avoided it last summer when Josh was fragile and needed to heal. Last night had seemed too soon and they'd been...busy. This morning felt no better when it came to timing. Yet to hide his relationship with Brad was wrong. And impossible. He wouldn't lie to Josh, even through avoidance.

But to actually say it, was difficult. The tension built in his chest. He became terrified that Josh would walk out in disgust, and Kir wouldn't blame him. His throat thickened and he couldn't quite speak.

"Kir?"

*Get a grip. Get a grip.*

"Hey." Josh pulled him down into his embrace but Kir looked away. Then Josh positioned himself on top, his length along Kir's, elbows above his shoulders. Josh brushed back Kir's hair, quieting him with touch. Gently Josh placed a hand beneath Kir's cheek and pushed, forcing him to either look into Josh's eyes or close his own.

Kir met Josh's gaze and saw concern.

"Your heart is going a mile a minute beneath me," said Josh. "What are you scared of?"

"I didn't know he'd go after you." Kir's voice shook.

"Why did he go after me?" Josh spoke as if he hadn't been brutalized by Brad.

"I stopped." Kir wished he could see Josh more clearly, wished he could stop speaking. But he owed Josh the truth. "I just couldn't be with Brad anymore. I'm so sorry." He felt helpless waiting for Josh to fling himself off the bed. But Josh kept stroking Kir's face, wiping away the tears.

"So you and Brad were together?"

Kir nodded.

"How long?"

Kir swallowed. "A year and a half. Off and on."

"Did he force you?"

Kir shook his head violently and closed his eyes, as if that would stop the tears. He waited for Josh to pull away in revulsion.

Instead, Josh lowered his mouth to Kir's eyelids and licked them, cleaning off the salt and the liquid around them, a soothing gesture that Kir had never experienced before Josh. After a while, Kir found he could stop crying.

He opened his eyes. Josh still waited above him, no disgust, his gaze honest and clear.

"Did he scare you, Kir?"

Kir smiled weakly. "I'm always a little scared."

"Are you scared now?"

"That you'll leave me. Now that you know."

Josh just watched. "But how did Brad know about me?"

"He met you, remember?"

Josh blinked, confused.

"You don't remember?"

"No."

It hadn't occurred to Kir that Brad would have prevented Josh from recognizing him. But it made sense. That way, Josh didn't tell the agency Brad was a Minder.

Josh's elbows began to shake.

"He must have messed with your memory," explained Kir. "You met him just before we parted three years ago. He knew I cared about you, though I tried to hide it. That was the problem."

They were both shaking now and Josh rolled onto his side, pulling Kir with him.

Kir spoke into Josh's shoulder. "Brad wouldn't have gone after you, except for me. He was angry that I wouldn't put out any longer."

"I think I'll blame Brad, not you," Josh ground out.

"I was frantic when you told me Brad was with you. I got to you as fast as I could."

Josh toyed with Kir's hair. "Somehow none of this surprises me. I think, at some level, I knew. Even if I can't remember."

There was a long silence.

"Did Brad hurt you, Kir?"

"Sometimes," he admitted.

"Did you like that?"

"Sometimes. Because I felt, I dunno, less culpable. A lie, but there you go."

Josh took a while to digest that, but he also pulled Kir closer. His caresses didn't stop and Kir couldn't stop clinging.

"Would you want me to hurt you?" Josh asked.

"I just want you."

"Good." Josh wrapped his hand carefully around Kir's cock. "Because I can't bring myself to hurt you."

Kir's tongue found Josh's nipple and soon Josh took control. Gently.

They showered and breakfasted—cereal with boxed milk. Kir was overwhelmed by his confession and Josh's forgiveness. It left him tongue-tied. So he made Josh coffee and himself tea.

"Thanks." Josh accepted the mug, a too-thoughtful expression on his face, and Kir braced himself. "I'm afraid we need to talk more. Though not, thankfully, about Brad."

Conversation had already exhausted Kir. Instead of talking, he wanted Josh to walk over and start touching him again, make everything feel right. Even if he already felt guilty that Josh gave more than he took when it came to sex. Kir could react but he couldn't take the initiative.

"Kir?" asked Josh and Kir nodded, ready to pay attention. "We can't stay here."

He stiffened. "You don't trust Trey?"

"No. I think our purposes, to date, have been similar, but that could change at any time. Trey could decide to lead Horton and his crew to our little hideaway."

"Let's get out." Kir stood, unable to enjoy his tea. Somehow he'd thought Josh trusted Trey more than this. "Now."

"Calm down. We should leave today, but I don't think Trey's about to bring us in yet. He's serious about helping us. Just the desire may not outlast other developments. There are people he's more interested in protecting."

"Still." Kir couldn't bear being back in the hands of the agency.

"We have a tiny problem of where to go, Kir. That's what we need to figure out."

"That's not a problem. I have a place."

Josh's jaw clenched. "As much as I like *you*, Kir, I cannot possibly hang out with a gang of Minders. All my hard-earned peace of mind will be shot to hell and I'll regress to the basket case I was last summer."

"No. No Minders and you weren't a basket case."

"A little unsteady, if I recall."

"No." Kir went to stand beside Josh.

To Kir's relief, Josh rose to embrace him. "What is this place of yours?" Josh said into his hair.

"An apartment a day's drive from here. It's my private place. My sister gave it to me when I needed to get away. No one else knows. And no one is stalking me, like Brad. I promise."

"You think it's safe."

"Safer than here."

♋ ♋ ♋

Josh watched Kir tell the car-rental guy they didn't need to pay for the car. Although Josh still had money from Brad, cash would draw more attention than Kir blurring the kid's mind so he wouldn't remember what they looked like. They drove out of the parking lot, Kir at the wheel. Apparently Maddie had decided Kir needed to learn to drive.

"You're not too tired from messing with the kid?" Josh asked with some concern.

"No, he didn't care if we paid or not. He's just doing a job."

"But he'll get in trouble later."

"Maybe," admitted Kir with a guilty glance at Josh.

Once they hit the highway, Josh thought of Maddie. Not his favorite person. "Is your sister worried about where you are?"

"I take off from time to time. She's probably happy to think I hooked up with Ted."

"God, no," said Josh, remembering Ed Harding. That scene in the bookstore was going to give him nightmares.

"She thinks I need to have sex more often." Kir flashed Josh an uncertain grin.

Josh smiled back. "Only with me."

Kir turned back to the road, looking pleased. "I'll let Maddie know I'm fine once we're settled."

"Don't tell her about me."

"Okay. She won't hurt you, you know."

Josh didn't know. In fact, he didn't think of Maddie as a particularly great sister.

"She knows how much I care about you." Kir tightened his grip on the steering wheel and Josh decided he wouldn't slag off the one person in the world who Kir had, besides himself.

"Okay."

"Your brother is worried about you," Kir said out of the blue, startling Josh.

"Who?"

Kir raised his eyebrows. "Your brother. Sam Mackay."

"He noticed I was gone?" Josh shook his head in disbelief. Sam, his feckless, self-centered younger brother, would have finished his year articling with some hotshot firm by now and didn't have time to think about fugitive family members.

"Uh, yeah, he noticed in a big way. Raised a stink."

"Sammy?" Josh knew he sounded slow on the uptake. His brother had taken Josh's phone calls while the agency held Josh prisoner, but Sam hadn't seemed interested. Or uninterested. Just bored. Perfunctory. Which was, Josh had to acknowledge, a family trait. "We're not close."

Kir looked puzzled. "You're close enough for him to ask why his adored older brother, who served in the marines for four years—I didn't know that, Josh—disappeared while in government custody." Kir was echoing Trey's earlier statements, which Josh found odd. "He's livid, Josh, and he's actually made it kind of awkward for the agency. Because he's an up-and-coming Washington lawyer with important friends. Going places. High-powered law firm. Apparently." Kir shrugged. "I don't really know about these things. This is what I gleaned from the internet."

Josh got worried. He didn't want his brother in trouble with the agency.

Kir noticed Josh's alarm. "Your brother isn't stupid. And he's not without connections. They can't really touch him for asking questions about you and demanding answers."

Josh turned and looked out the window, overcome by Sam's apparent concern. "He was such a brat, Kir, you wouldn't believe it."

"Yeah? Well, I guess older brothers often think that."

"Especially when the mother spoils the kid rotten."

"Your mother didn't spoil you?"

Josh paused. "No. She couldn't. She was dead. Sam's my half-brother. His mother didn't like me much."

"How could she not like you?" Kir's naive amazement warmed Josh.

"You are too sweet."

Kir blushed. Josh liked making Kir blush. His dark skin got darker and redder. His eyes brightened with pleasure.

They talked on and off for the rest of the day. Mostly Kir reassuring Josh that a horde of Minders wouldn't descend upon them, or Josh trying out different long-term survival scenarios. He seemed to think they should winter in an abandoned state park. Kir would do anything for Josh, but rather hoped it wouldn't come to that. Josh had become too hard and skinny this past year and Kir wanted to look after him. Winter camping meant Josh looking after Kir when Josh already did too much for Kir.

They arrived at dusk, pulling into the underground parking lot. He could feel Josh's tension wafting off him. Kir got them out of the parking lot, up the elevator and into the apartment.

Kir poured them drinks while Josh prowled the small space, checking out the bedroom, bathroom and kitchen, before stopping to stare out the window in the living room.

"Nice skyline," he said as Kir offered him water. Josh didn't drink alcohol or Kir would have opened a bottle of wine to help him relax. Maybe touch would help. Josh's touch always helped Kir.

A little shyly, Kir leaned his head against Josh and Josh's arm came around Kir's shoulders, pulling him close for a kiss on the forehead. Kir liked that he could touch Josh now instead of guarding against any inadvertent contact. But it also made him nervous. Kir should sometimes make the first move and he didn't quite know how.

He knew how to respond. He learned that too well, even if he loved reacting to Josh and his hands, his lips, his tongue.

"What is going on in that pretty head of yours?" asked Josh.

Kir felt his face suffuse with heat, with pleasure. He adored Josh's casual compliments and endearments. Over the past year, he had taken out memories of such instances and hugged them close when he'd felt so alone. Last summer, Josh hadn't been comfortable enough to say such things easily, yet he'd called Kir babe twice, and Kir had treasured both times.

Josh's fingers brushed the back of Kir's neck and he shivered. "Now what exactly did your sister say about you and sex?"

Kir smiled, looking down, wishing he could say something sexy and complimentary but phrases like, *you mean so much to me*, or, *I love you*, sounded stupid to his ears. So he said nothing, a dumb mute.

Josh downed his glass. "Let's work up an appetite." They'd picked up Chinese food.

"Okay," said Kir in a low, eager voice, in case his silence put Josh off.

Then Josh was undressing Kir who trembled with anticipation.

"You are so beautiful."

Kir just stared, drowning in Josh's eyes.

"Kir, promise me you won't let anyone hurt you again."

"Just you," Kir managed because his brain seemed to be lacking air.

Josh stiffened. "I won't. I refuse to hurt you."

"I just want to be with you," Kir elaborated. "No one else."

Josh relaxed then and his hands danced over Kir until Kir lay in his arms and they made love.

Later they sat on the living-room floor naked, eating noodles and chicken balls in the dark, the city lights their only guide.

"These taste like shit," declared Josh, losing interest in most of his meal.

"You need to eat more. I'll cook tomorrow."

"You will, will you?"

"After I shop."

Josh swallowed his mouthful. "How long do we plan on staying here anyway?"

Kir frowned. "A few weeks should be safe."

"And our strategy to bring the agency down. What about that?"

Kir looked at Josh in surprise. "What strategy?"

"That's the problem," Josh said grimly, and Kir regretted losing Josh's warmth. "We need a fucking plan. We can't just be on the run, because then they'll chase us."

"Well, I have been doing a bit of work."

Josh's gaze sharpened. "Work?"

"Sending stuff to newspapers. Stuff that can be verified."

"You be careful. They'll trace you."

"I'm not stupid."

"I would never think you're stupid, Kir."

Kir looked away, embarrassed.

"Who called you stupid?" asked Josh.

"Snow," Kir spat. His guardian, his handler, his pedophile lover. His leg began jigging up and down.

"I'm glad I killed him."

Kir shot Josh a questioning look. "Are you? I didn't think you were."

"After a long winter to think things over, I decided, yes, I was glad to have killed Snow. And Brad." Josh expression hardened. "Despite their best efforts, I didn't kill you or even bring you in."

Kir crawled over and buried himself in Josh, pressing his face against Josh's neck. Josh held him and they rested like that for a while. Kir could caress Josh now that they were both sated and he didn't have to worry about how the sex was scripted. Normal sex, that was. He felt like he had so much to learn in this relationship.

He listened to Josh's heartbeat, then nuzzled the pulse in Josh's throat. Kir's hands drifted down, counting ribs, finding Josh's hipbones, enjoying the sensation of exploring Josh's body with no hurry, no agenda. Josh had less body hair than Kir, but Kir liked the feel of the hair that did dust Josh's skin. He should explain all this to Josh, but he found it difficult to articulate so he just kissed Josh's breastbone.

Beneath him, Josh hardened and Kir went breathless, wishing the slow exploration wasn't ending, yet anticipating what would come next.

Josh breathed hot air in his ear. "Just what are you trying to do here, Kir? Wear me out?"

Kir rose up. "You don't have to do anything."

Josh rubbed Kir's arms. "Hey, come back here. I like you attached to me."

Kir ducked his head back down. Josh's warm hand came round to massage Kir's neck, then raised his face so they were looking at each other.

"You prefer touching me more after sex, than before," Josh observed.

"No." Or at least, it was more complicated than that.

Josh traced Kir's lips. "Don't look stricken. This isn't a critique, Kir. Everyone has their likes and dislikes. Even me."

Josh rolled Kir on his back and held him down, his expression intense. "Or were you just toying with me earlier?"

"Toying?" Kir queried.

Josh looked serious, but amusement lurked in his gray eyes. "You want to touch, you have to pay." Then Josh overwhelmed him with touch and mouth and cock and Kir submitted to sensation.

Kir woke in bed. They'd dragged themselves there, leaving Chinese leftovers on the floor. But Josh had already risen and Kir decided Josh needed to sleep more, as well as eat more.

After breakfast, they discussed which newspapers Kir had approached and how. Josh was impressed by the way Kir had covered his tracks, making Kir glow inside. That turned Josh on and Kir sucked him off because Josh had decided that Kir's backside needed a break. Kir didn't argue. Although he could never have enough of Josh's cock, he was sore and tender.

Josh surprised Kir by taking him in his mouth at the same time. Later they lay entwined, Kir drawing patterns on Josh's chest, Kir kissing Josh's neck, Kir rolling on top of Josh and licking his mouth until Josh laughed and opened for his kiss.

"After you leave me—" Kir stopped. Why did he have to say that? It was one of his many fears, but that didn't mean he had to blurt it out. He needed to *think* first.

Beneath him, Josh stilled and his face became blank, which unnerved Kir.

"I'm leaving you." Josh used his flat tone that hid everything. "Why? What do you know that I don't?"

Kir had scared Josh. He didn't want to do that. Ever. "No." He gave Josh urgent kisses. "I just mean, you know, we might not last."

At that, Josh looked baffled. "You're already planning our breakup?"

"No."

"Then what?"

"You'll get tired of me," Kir said lamely, unable to say the appropriate thing to end a conversation he should not have started.

"I will? Huh." Josh spoke as if Kir had revealed an interesting fact to him. "I've never had sex so often in my life. What cues are you picking up that I'm likely to tire of you?"

"I'm a freak," Kir burst out because Josh looked offended.

Josh watched him, but his expression relaxed and Kir let out a breath of relief.

"I'm sorry. I didn't mean to say it aloud. I'm always scared of the future, but from now on I'll shut up."

"Better to speak." Josh touched Kir's face gently, as he always did when he wanted to soothe. "I like to know what's going on behind those gorgeous eyes of yours." Josh closed Kir's eyes with his thumbs, then traced the bone below Kir's lashes.

"No one has ever responded to me like you do. But maybe it means less to you?" Josh asked.

"You mean everything to me," Kir whispered.

"Okay," said Josh. "Okay." And he smiled.

# Chapter Five

They lasted a week on their own. Josh felt like all he did was eat and have sex, as if he'd been starved of both and couldn't get enough. He also slept a fair amount because sex relaxed him. Kir, of course, slept with him.

He watched Kir, to make sure he wanted every touch, caress and fuck Josh gave him. Kir's history of handing himself over, as his pervert guardian had taught him, scared Josh a little. It was a concern and the onus was on Josh to handle Kir with care.

Yet Kir was light with joy. As was he, Josh supposed, after that grim winter. He felt light-years different from last summer, though he'd lived with Kir then, and made love to him. Something inside had healed. The scar still felt tender, but it held.

Face-to-face, Josh shuddered, coming inside Kir. As he leaned forward to kiss Kir on the mouth, someone walked into the apartment and Josh went rigid, his hazy post-sex high shattered.

"Kir?" yelled a woman as Josh pulled out in shock.

"It's okay." Kir wrapped himself around Josh. "It's Maddie."

"Shit." Panic bloomed in Josh's chest. After his winter in the park, he'd thought to be past his fear. What bullshit.

"It's okay," repeated Kir. "Don't come in here," he yelled as his sister approached the open bedroom door and he yanked the cover over Josh.

She marched right in. "You idiot, Kir. How could you bring a total stranger..." Her mouth hung open for a moment. "Is that Josh?"

Kir climbed over Josh. "Get the fuck out. I'll be with you in a moment."

"Okay, okay." She backed up, making an exaggerated show of shielding her eyes. "I thought you'd brought that Ted guy here."

Kir turned to look apologetically at Josh who breathed easier now that he'd seen Maddie. At least she acted more like a sister than a Minder. The last time they'd met, she'd forced him into her car so she could drink tea with him.

"Stay here, Josh." Kir pulled on jeans and stalked out of the bedroom.

Josh lay there, hearing them argue, but could not make out the words. He chose not be scared of Maddie. No point. Either Kir's love would keep Maddie's fucking words out of his head, or it wouldn't. Time to find out.

Josh dressed, took a deep breath and walked out. As he entered the living room, they stopped talking. At once, Kir came to him, standing close and slightly in front. Maddie gave Josh the once-over. "You're looking at me as if I'm the grim reaper, Josh."

"Well, the last time Josh saw you, Maddie, you were—"

"Yes, yes." Maddie waved her hand in irritation, then turned her gaze back to Josh who tried not to flinch. "Don't worry, Kir will either eat me alive or, worse, get hysterical if I mess with you. So I won't."

"Don't be a bitch," said Kir. Josh placed a hand on his shoulder, trying to calm him. "The last time—"

"The last time you came within a hundred miles of me, you led Brad to us," Josh finished, though he suspected Kir had planned to refer to the tea party Maddie had held for Josh.

Maddie blinked. "I'm sorry about that. Although it kinda worked out in the end. You killed Brad. I've decided that's a good thing."

"Really?" Josh wasn't impressed. "It is a good thing. Brad liked to hurt Kir."

She sighed.

"Josh," protested Kir.

Maddie faced Josh's glare. "I don't interfere in my brother's sex life. If I did, you wouldn't be here."

"Such a protective older sister. I especially like the way you abandoned him when he was twelve."

She sneered which told Josh he'd made a direct hit.

Kir stepped between them. "Look, guys, that's really enough."

Because Kir was anxious, Josh held his tongue. He wanted to tell Maddie she was one shitty sister. Later, perhaps.

"It's good to see you're so attached to Kir," said Maddie. "Though why you'd take off last summer—"

"Maddie, *shut up*," demanded Kir.

"I'd never seen Kir so happy," she continued blithely on, "as he had been with you and then, *poof*, you had vanished. No forwarding address."

Josh pulled Kir back and wrapped him in his arms. Kir leaned into him, covering his arms with his own.

Over Kir's shoulder, Josh stared at Maddie. "It's just the kind of flighty guy I am. If I think I might slice open my lover's heart with a knife, I take off. *Poof.*"

Maddie paled, giving Josh some satisfaction. She hadn't known just how dangerous Brad was for Kir.

"Not that this urge strikes me often. In fact, it only happens when a fucking Minder tells me to kill Kir." Josh's voice had gone harsh, but he didn't care. Kir was in his arms, Maddie looked shocked and he, Josh, only wanted Kir to be safe.

"You're stronger than you look, Josh Mackay." Maddie marched off to the kitchen and ran water, getting something to drink. Kir turned in Josh's arms and kissed his neck.

"She's really angry with me," Kir murmured. "Because she didn't know where I was. I should have contacted her."

Josh shrugged. He'd rather Maddie, an unknown quantity, still didn't know anything. But he supposed Kir and Maddie wanted some brother-sister time and Josh didn't need to be around her.

"Don't stay up too late," Josh told Kir and went to bed.

Maddie stayed for a few days and Kir made it a point not to leave Josh alone with her. Just as well considering the conversations she and Josh tended to have.

"I gather you punched Kir last summer," said Maddie, out of the blue. "He had the remnants of a shiner when he came to town. Said he walked into a door. He's a terrible liar."

Josh looked at Kir, remembering when he feared Kir was controlling him. When Kir had only wanted Josh's company. "I wish I hadn't hit you."

Kir's dark eyes melted and Josh's stomach swooped low. If Maddie wasn't sitting in their living room...

"It didn't matter," claimed Kir.

"It *mattered*," said Josh with feeling. "I like to think my head was still foggy from my time with Brad, but I wish I'd trusted you."

Maddie jumped up, shaking her head. "I'm going for a walk. Be done within an hour."

"Huh?" Though Kir didn't try to stop her.

Josh prowled over to Kir's side of the couch and breathed in his scent before kissing him.

"Oh." Kir smiled now and Josh wondered how he couldn't have known why Maddie had left. But Kir's experiences were unique and, for the most part, uniquely bad.

"Don't say it didn't matter."

"Okay."

"It really bothered me."

"I know, I know. I just meant that I understood why." Kir stroked Josh's unshaved cheek. "You were frightened, Josh."

"Yeah. I was." He'd been terrified.

Josh gathered Kir in his arms and kissed him.

"Do you mind leading all the time?" Kir asked.

Josh pulled back and cocked his head. "Care to elaborate?"

"In sex, you'll get tired of me just, you know, responding."

Josh's regarded Kir steadily. "Who told you that?"

Kir's gaze darted away, then back. He hadn't wanted to name Brad but Josh guessed.

"Brad was a complete asshole, you know that." Josh kissed Kir again. "Let me tell you something. I *like* being in control. I've had boyfriends break off with me because I like it too much. But I'll work on it with you, so that doesn't happen with us."

"I'm not going to leave you, Josh," Kir said, amazed at the idea.

Josh just smiled as if he knew better and Kir felt indignant. Josh didn't understand how much he meant to Kir. He pushed Josh's shoulder in protest and Josh glanced down, eyebrows raised.

Kir became irritated. "You don't *want* to know how unlikely it is that I would leave you. I watch what I say, so you don't think you have a barnacle stuck to you."

Josh grabbed Kir's hand and dragged him to the bedroom where the condoms and lube lay. As he efficiently divested Kir of his clothing, he said, "You need to stay with me so I can fuck you whenever I want, Kir. Bend over."

Without preamble, Josh entered Kir who grunted, trying to catch up to speed. Josh pulled out, Kir hardened and Josh plunged again, then stilled. He brought Kir up and back to lean against him, pinched Kir's nipple and massaged Kir's balls till Kir thought his head would explode with the sensation of Josh inside him and all around him. Just before Kir was about to come, Josh went motionless.

"Josh," he pleaded.

"Were you trying to tell me, in your roundabout way, that you don't want to bottom?"

"*What?*" Was Josh teasing?

"No?" There was a smile in Josh's voice.

He pushed Kir forward again, so he was on hands and knees, then pulled out and slammed into Kir.

"Answer me, Kir." Josh retreated, thrust, developing rhythm and Kir could only gasp, so close to the edge and shivering with need.

"Kir," Josh warned.

"Christ, Josh, I want this."

"So. Do. I." Josh swore, coming inside Kir who just managed not to collapse. He loved the feel of Josh's orgasm within him. Even as the last of Josh pulsed, he nipped Kir's neck and his hand grasped Kir's cock, urging Kir on. Kir groaned, falling forward and letting go, though Josh didn't let go as Kir spurted through Josh's fingers.

When Kir stopped shuddering, Josh turned him over and mock-glared at him. "I will never get tired of you responding. I expect you to respond whenever I damned please."

Kir grinned up, then pulled Josh down for a kiss.


Later that day, while Kir showered, Maddie announced she was leaving. She pinned her gaze on Josh. "You'll be glad."

"Sure," Josh agreed. Kir didn't expect Josh and Maddie to get along. Kir seemed to believe Maddie could care about fellow Minders, but no one else.

She ripped off a hunk of fresh bread and chewed on it. "Do you mind explaining why you loathe me? I can feel your disapproval wafting off you and coming right at me."

Josh smiled tightly. "Where to begin?"

"You tell me."

*You're the crappiest sister I've ever met,* wasn't quite specific enough. Besides, he didn't make sweeping statements that hurt Kir. Crappy or not, Maddie had been the one person in Kir's life to show some kind of concern for him over the years. Even if that concern was ineffective, if not downright harmful.

"Well," offered Josh, "this visit hasn't been quite so bad, seeing as you didn't bring a psychopath along."

Maddie nodded. "Yes, Brad followed me last summer. I apologized for that."

"Oh, you apologized. Well then, everything's okay. No harm done. But wait. Harm *was* done. I was given this strange idea to kill Kir."

Maddie rolled her eyes. "It's over. I can't exactly fix it now. But you know, I don't think that's what you dislike about me."

She was right. The real source of his anger came from that much earlier event he'd already referred to. "You left Kir at the agency when he was twelve years old." Josh didn't bother to hide his contempt. "He couldn't defend himself."

Maddie's facade did not fail her. She looked as nonchalant as ever, but the stiffness in her shoulders hadn't been there before. She gave him a slight smile, no humor in it.

"I was naive. Funny what a warped place that fucking agency was. I didn't even know men fucked boys. I thought they only fucked girls. Like me."

*Crap.* If Josh had thought it through, he might have wondered what they'd done to Maddie.

"And yet they did," said Josh, though the fight was no longer in him. Maddie's abuse didn't exonerate her, but he found it hard to keep beating this horse. Besides, the water had stopped running. Kir had ended his shower.

Maddie's brown gaze turned icy, in a way Kir's never did. "You're right, I abandoned Kir, who continued on in my stead, till I could rescue him. And then, for a number of years, he refused to stay with me. He didn't forgive me until after he met you, in fact."

Josh didn't know what to make of that.

"Not such a fun conversation, is it? Though you're not without your own sordid past now." Her voice softened. "I'm glad you actually care about Kir. He's very emotional."

At that moment Kir stalked out of the bathroom, glaring at Maddie. "Do you mind? You don't have to lecture Josh about my flaws."

Josh reached out and pulled a wet Kir to him. "Babe, you have no flaws."

Kir looked down, smiling.

"Well, if nothing else, you're very cute together." This time Maddie's smile was real and to Josh's surprise he saw an echo of Kir in her expression. He had thought they shared their deeply brown eyes and nothing else.

Then her face went serious. "I just told Josh a little about Horton, Kir."

Kir nodded, then glanced at Josh who'd gone stiff beside him.

"*Horton?*" Josh looked at Maddie.

"He was my handler. Literally. What a fucker. Literally." Maddie's nonchalant pose didn't convince anyone. A tremor passed through her.

Josh felt his mouth quiver with distaste. "Three years ago Horton hired me to bring in Kir. But I—Christ." He shook his head. "Horton is obsessed with Minders."

"We know," said Maddie.

Josh, now appalled, withdrew from Kir and rubbed his temples. He and Kir had been living in a fantasyland this past week, but now all those god-awful worries came flooding back. The agency wanted Kir and Josh. And perhaps Maddie.

♋ ♋ ♋

That afternoon Maddie left and Josh prowled around the apartment, feeling caged. Only Kir went outside, because he could smudge his own existence more easily than Josh's. People didn't really see Kir.

When he returned, Josh jumped him and Kir fought back. He didn't have Josh's height, but their weight was not so different—Josh knew he was too thin. At one point Kir pinned Josh to the ground and forced a kiss upon him. Josh responded, letting Kir keep control of the kiss until Kir lost his guard. Josh took advantage and flipped Kir flat on his back while Kir hooted. As he struggled to rise, Josh turned Kir around and held him in an armlock while Josh prepped for entry.

"You want it," he told Kir who just grunted as Josh toyed with his hole. Then he slammed inside.

"God," said Kir who gave up the fight for fucking.

It brought relief and joy not to treat each other with kid gloves and they ended up laughing a lot afterwards while Kir explored Josh's sated body with a curiosity Josh found endearing.

Later still, they lay and talked.

"I don't know how long I can stay in a one-bedroom apartment. The first week was fine, a refreshing change after my winter outside. But I'm beginning to feel a little claustrophobic. And"—Josh cleared his throat—"that brings back bad memories."

Kir pressed kisses on his face, then pulled back. "The stationary bike isn't enough, I guess."

Josh observed Kir's wry expression and responded in kind. "Somehow, I know I'm not outside, or even moving."

"I'm sorry about Maddie."

Josh took a deep breath. "Well, I don't dislike her quite as much, so perhaps the visit wasn't a complete loss."

"She's all I've got, except you." Kir stared at Josh's shoulder. "I can't let her go."

Josh sank his fingers into Kir's unruly hair. "I don't want you to. You don't need to choose between us, Kir, even if we don't get along."

After dinner, they were cleaning up the kitchen when someone knocked on the door. They both froze.

"Maddie?" Josh said in an undertone. Kir shook his head, as if her return didn't make sense. They walked to the door and Kir peered through the peephole.

"Trey," Kir mouthed and Trey said, "That's right, it's me. Open the door before I draw attention to you."

Josh wondered if Trey's exceptionality was super-hearing or mind-reading while Kir unlocked the door.

But Trey didn't walk in. He stood in the doorway, looking at them with an expression Josh had never seen on Trey's face— regret. It unnerved Josh.

He glanced at Kir who swallowed, his face tightening. "Trey, you don't want to be here."

Trey smiled without humor. "Your magic doesn't work on me, buddy. Sorry. I'm a freak, too."

"Does Horton know that?" Josh tried to figure out what had prompted this visit while hoping to engage Trey, who seemed remote despite his regret.

The agent shook his head, but whether as an answer to Josh's question, he didn't know. "You would have been safer at my place. I guess it was too much to expect you'd trust me on that. This way I had to find you by following Maddie and, well, the agency became too interested in my search."

"We have to leave."

Again, Trey shook his head. "It's too late, Josh."

Kir's teeth began to chatter and Josh wrapped an arm around him, all the while looking at Trey. "You are going to help us," said Josh.

"I will," agreed Trey. "But first you'll be taken into custody."

Kir moaned.

"I'll go public." Josh offered Trey what he'd wanted back at the park. "I'll talk to whoever you think I should talk to. I'll tell them everything."

"You're surrounded," Trey explained. "And not by the media, I'm afraid. The agency."

"You're handing us over." Josh couldn't believe it. He hadn't expected this blatant a betrayal when they'd run from Trey's safe house.

"I have no choice. I couldn't hide your location from them. My powers are quite limited."

"What do they think you're doing now?"

Trey's smile was grim. "Convincing you to leave with me. It's Kir they want to restrain."

"*No*," said Josh.

"I told them you'd be under Kir's influence—"

"I'm *not*—"

Trey kept talking. "—but Horton thought I should check. Since you once worked for him." Trey stepped back.

"Look, Trey—" began Josh.

"Get down. Cover your ears."

Josh started towards him and Trey pulled a gun. He opened his hand, an apologetic shrug, then backed out of their apartment, shutting the door. Josh heard the warning whine and dragged Kir down, covering him. The window broke and the explosion knocked Josh out.

# Chapter Six

His head pounding, Kir faded in and out of consciousness. Despite the haze of pain, he recognized the room.

The punishment room, Snow used to call it. Where Kir was banished when he didn't cooperate, which wasn't all that often. The windowless room, dismal and gray, had filled Kir with dread and besides, he had been eager to please Snow.

Someone—not Snow who was dead three years now—had been kind enough to bring in a cot upon which he lay. Kir tried to rise but the old memories made him shake and he had to lie down.

He passed out again and woke next with a terrible thirst. He'd been drugged he now realized. Part of the reason he felt groggy and far from alert. The explosion hadn't helped either.

"Kiran Brunner."

Kir jumped at the voice coming through the speaker. Though it didn't belong to Snow, but Horton, a man who had visited frequently during Kir's last years with the agency.

"Good morning," added Horton.

Kir wondered which morning and how long he'd been out. Then he closed his eyes as he remembered Josh had been with him. Unlikely that Josh had escaped. He would have taken the noise bomb harder than Kir, because Josh had protected Kir with his body and covered Kir's ears with his hands.

Trey had betrayed them.

"Josh Mackay is in our custody," said Horton. Kir didn't doubt it, but found it painful to hear. "His good health will depend on your good behavior. Do you understand?"

Kir lay there, in despair.

"You had better get up and nod that head of yours, Kir. For Josh's sake, if not yours."

Kir pushed himself up.

"Listen to me carefully. I am going to come in and talk to you. I realize you're weak but I know you. I know you can manipulate me. Someone will be monitoring us and if they see you misuse your powers, they will intervene and Josh will suffer." Horton let that last word echo. "So, Kir, can I come in and you won't molest my mind?"

Kir hung his head in a semblance of a nod.

In less than a minute, Horton pushed the thick door open and shut it behind him. He stood an inch taller than Kir, with thinning hair and a grizzled beard. Intelligent eyes. Maddie had warned Kir Horton wasn't stupid.

Horton stood there, shaking his head. "You don't look much like your sister, you know that?"

Kir rubbed his bleary eyes. He hoped the drug wore off soon, because he needed his wits about him, such as they were.

Horton sat on the chair in the corner. "How are you feeling?"

"Not great." Kir didn't want to answer Horton's questions, didn't want to talk. But Kir had to be as compliant as possible. It was his way to get around people.

"Is there anything I can get you?"

"I need to piss and I'm thirsty."

Horton looked into the camera and nodded. "They'll bring you a drink." He gestured to the corner. "The hole is there."

Wearily, Kir relieved himself on camera, in front of Horton. He supposed he could be grateful Horton's interest wasn't sexual, but gratitude was a difficult emotion to summon. Still they delivered the drink and Kir sat on the cot with a large bottle of water and guzzled it.

Horton watched him drink, which made his skin crawl. Horton's pale blue eyes seemed slightly dead.

Sitting back, Horton crossed his legs. "So, I want to tell you something."

Kir nodded.

"Josh doesn't interest me very much. Truth be told, I'm still irritated by his interference three years ago."

Kir blinked, trying to read the meaning behind his words.

"When he helped you escape," Horton explained.

"That was my fault," Kir said quickly. "I used him."

"How gallant of you to take responsibility for his actions. The point is, I've only ever tried to use Josh to get to you. I will continue to do so. If you use your powers against me, or the agency, Josh will be punished."

Kir found it hard to breathe, but he nodded again. *Puppet, puppet.*

"Do you understand? I'm thinking a bit of finger-breaking, to start. It can get much worse. Eyes are always vulnerable."

Kir began to shake and Horton smiled.

"Unlike Snow, I'm not fond of sexual torture. But I am just as ruthless. Even if, personally, I have nothing against Josh. In fact, I like him."

Kir tried not to let his lip curl in disgust.

"Do you understand?"

"Yes," whispered Kir.

"Good. Because I am happy to keep Josh in the best of health." Horton smiled as if he expected Kir to smile back. "Tell me, how is your hearing, Kir? Any damage?"

"I'm fine." His head hurt, but he didn't think his hearing had been affected.

"Excellent. I don't want you deaf. You wouldn't be as useful. And you're going to be very useful, aren't you?"

"I am," said Kir fervently. He was also going to rescue Josh, he just didn't know how. Rescuing Josh from Brad had been easy. Maddie had planned it. She had brains. Kir didn't. At least, not when frightened. And he was very frightened now. It no doubt showed.

Horton laughed. "My goodness, so eager. But then, Snow was your handler. He wanted you docile, pliant, lacking in spirit. Because otherwise you might do as your sister did, and get away from us. And you never did, at least not on your own."

"Where's Josh?"

"Ah, you're more interested in talking about Josh than yourself. I suppose that makes sense."

Kir swallowed.

"He's not too far away. I can't be more specific than that."

Kir pulled in a shaky breath. "What exactly do you want of me?"

Horton smiled again. "I want you to save the agency, Kir."

"How?"

"If I say jump, will you say how high? Did Snow really program you that well?"

"I think so," admitted Kir, remembering how Snow had delighted in praising Kir for being feisty and spirited, when they both knew Kir had neither quality.

"God knows what Josh sees in you. I mean, nice body, I'm sure—not that men attract me."

*Yes, yes.*

"But what normal man would want to be with you, freak and whore that you are? Trash, really. Yet Josh seems genuinely concerned about you. You were the first person he asked about when he regained consciousness."

Kir's face heated up.

"Ah, that information affects you. It is so convenient you care."

"Will you tell me what you want?"

Horton regarded Kir. "Okay. Let me give it to you in a nutshell—you're going to talk to a number of important people and make their doubts about the agency vanish."

"How can they talk to me if I'm in this room?"

"You won't be. Once I'm convinced you're obedient, you'll become my new assistant, at least in name. You'll come to a rendezvous, convince our target you should remain at the table to chat and then make a couple of forceful statements."

"It doesn't always work."

"Don't play me for stupid, Kir. I know Snow used you often for this type of thing. Now, he wanted people to give him money for no reason they could comprehend, or he wanted to blackmail someone, but you managed quite well back then. Snow died with a tidy sum of money."

Kir felt sick to his stomach.

"What? Not good memories?"

"No."

"Well, it is different now. There is Josh to consider."

"Yes," agreed Kir. "But how do I know Josh is alive?"

"We'll let you see him on video."

"You could fake it."

"Nah, we'll set it up so you can ask him a question. How well he's able to answer will depend on you, of course."

Kir teared up. Josh would end up dead unless Kir was extremely careful. He didn't think he could survive Josh's death, not when it was caused by his very existence.

"Your sister never cried," said Horton.

*No, and Maddie still doesn't cry. She doesn't have sex now either. Doesn't care for anyone, except me and a few Minders.*

Horton stood and hiked up his pants. "Before we get started, you'll need a day or two to recover from the shock of being back here. You're too pale. You'll also need to be fitted for the job. Dirty shirt and jeans won't convince anyone you're my assistant. Someone will be in to measure you."

"Okay."

Horton left after a few more comments about Josh's health and Kir's goodwill. A bit later food arrived followed by a nervous man who measured Kir while Kir gritted his teeth.

Then Kir crawled back onto the cot and escaped to sleep.

♋ ♋ ♋

Next visit, Horton brought a laptop. When Kir opened it, he saw Josh, live on camera, pacing his room like a caged animal. Kir's heart stopped at the bleak expression on Josh's face. He disliked being closed in. More than Kir who had, at least, grown up with it. He knew how to adapt.

Kir looked up at Horton. "You said I could talk to him."

"Josh refuses to talk to you." Horton shrugged. "We didn't think forcing the issue was in Josh's best interest, but if that's what you want you'll get it."

"No," said Kir, unsure if Horton lied or not. Josh might refuse to cooperate in any way. Or he might be angry with Kir, but Kir rejected that possibility.

Horton had a small smile on his face. "You'd think Josh would be more grateful. We told him you wanted to talk to him. That you needed his reassurance. All he said, so eloquently, was, 'Fuck you.'"

Kir looked away so Horton wouldn't be able to read his face. He probably showed all his insecurities and longing and fear. Fear for Josh, fear that Josh hated him.

"In fact, Josh doesn't seem to like you much anymore." Horton seemed to see right through to Kir. "But that's not important. What's important is that *you* like *Josh*."

*Josh likes me*, Kir wanted to shout, but he just kept his eyes glued on Josh prowling his room, shedding excess energy, losing weight again.

"I'll take the computer," said Horton and Kir relinquished his link to Josh. "Now we'll get you prepped for a first meeting. This one's not critical. We just want to see how you function in the field."

Kir went through the motions without thinking. Like old times. They cut his hair. He showered and dressed. They groomed him. Horton watched with a knowing eye, apparently pleased. At least Horton had no desire to kiss him as Snow had.

The first man Kir met, a friend of Horton's, was troubled by some of the agency's antics, as he named them. As if the agency was a recalcitrant child that had to be brought to heel. Kir surprised the friend by joining them for drinks. When Kir "reminded" the man he wanted to meet Horton's new assistant, they became a friendly party of three.

Kir remained quiet while the other two talked about old times, new times, agency goals. At the right moment, Kir ventured that the agency did a good job under difficult circumstances—these had been Horton's words—and the friend's brow creased. There was less resistance than Kir expected. Though Kir didn't think he had just saved the agency, he had shut down a questioning voice and it made him sick—he had acted against himself.

He found he couldn't finish his drink, his head was swimming.

"Your assistant looks a little pale," the friend observed. Shortly thereafter Horton decided they should leave.

Kir feared Horton would be angry Kir hadn't hid his unease but, in the limo on the way home, Horton grinned, flushed with success. Giddy, and Kir remembered the old days when Snow would literally crow in the backseat, thinking there was nothing he couldn't accomplish with Kir at his side or on his lap or in whatever position Snow chose.

Horton let Kir slump in his own seat and he proved a little more observant than Snow had been. "What's wrong?" he asked, reining in his exuberance.

"It always makes me a little sick," Kir acknowledged, seeing no reason to hide it.

"With so few words? You hardly said a thing."

Kir nodded.

Horton eyed him. "Your sister could accomplish much more."

"She's not here." Thank God. In this situation, Maddie would kill herself.

"No. Not that I could count on her. One day she'd obey and the next she'd do her own thing." Horton paused. "I found something admirable in that. It's better, though, that Snow broke your spirit. If you ever had any."

Kir looked out the window.

On the outside, Kir felt like a machine, a very obedient machine. But on the inside, he was watching. Nobody could know about the inside. He guarded himself and waited.

In the week that followed, Kir worked on four other men with similar levels of success. He took more care to hide his discomfort, to wait until he got back to his room to be sick.

Horton praised him. Kir was appalled that the praise at some level pleased him. What was the matter with him? He told himself he just wanted Josh to be safe. But his actions hurt people. At some point—soon, he hoped—he would have to undermine Horton's efforts, all the while protecting Josh. Kir feared he didn't have the strength and resources to play that double game.

He had nightmares he couldn't remember and woke terrified of the unknown. He had to find his opening and until then, obey. The waiting was painful because he didn't know what opportunity would present itself and he feared it wouldn't arrive, or worse, he wouldn't recognize it.

Then one morning, Trey paid him a visit. The large man walked through the door. His very presence startled Kir who'd been expecting Horton.

"Jumpy?" asked Trey, his voice flat, his face turned to stone.

Kir backed up to a wall. Trey. Betrayal.

Trey's face became even more unreadable. Its blank grimness frightened Kir. Trey planned to physically threaten him. Kir recognized the type.

Instead, Trey began to pace. Kir wanted to fade into the wall to escape Trey's silent presence. The pacing made Kir think of Josh, last seen by Kir over video, sleeping on the cot. Horton claimed Josh was not drugged, but one of Josh's hands had been scraped and his face was bruised.

Trey came to a stop and turned. "You realize that Josh hates you."

Kir jerked his head up. The words hurt.

"After you shot Ed Harding, Josh had no choice but to do exactly what you wanted. You cannot be surprised at his hate. This is the third time you've taken control of him. At your apartment, he wouldn't even leave you to come with me."

Kir continued to stare straight ahead, his thoughts whirring. *Don't show it,* don't show that Trey made no sense whatsoever. Trey *knew* Josh had chosen to be with Kir. Josh had shot Ed. Trey had driven the getaway car.

"I wouldn't mind some kind of response here. Horton says you're very obedient."

"I'm obedient," Kir parroted.

"Good. It's important to know when to obey."

Kir looked up at Trey whose stone expression had vanished. His voice remained conversational and slightly sinister, but his eyes burned with meaning, as if something mattered very much indeed.

Trey resumed pacing. "Horton didn't want to explain that Josh hates you. But you need an explanation for why Josh won't talk to you. Otherwise you will balk when it is most important."

These statements that Josh hated Kir were false. They were Josh's way of telling Kir not to help the agency. He watched Trey, trying to read his message.

"You'll meet Josh's brother soon. That's why I'm here, to prepare you."

"Prepare me?" Kir's heart began to hammer. Josh's brother. He didn't want to manipulate Josh's brother. Josh had described Sam as a brat, but with some affection.

Kir swore he saw concern behind Trey's grim expression, but he had trouble making sense of the situation. He'd never had a cool head under pressure.

"I am in charge of Josh's well-being," Trey informed him. "I decide what happens if you don't behave. So when they take you to Sam Mackay, make sure you do the right thing." Then Trey did what Kir had been waiting for ever since Trey had entered the room. He walked up and grabbed Kir, hauling him off the ground to slam him against the wall. Kir began gulping in air.

Trey's face pushed up against Kir's, his pale blue eyes intense and unflinching.

*Tell,* Trey mouthed, then released him. Kir dropped to the floor as Trey strode out. Kir folded into himself, burying his head in his arms, and rocked a little, hiding his face from the camera.

*Tell.*

Kir wished he had good reason to trust Trey.

♋ ♋ ♋

The next day Horton came in and looked over a well-groomed Kir with approval. "I would have been ticked off if Trey had bruised you."

"My back hurts."

"Your back doesn't show." Horton paused. "Yesterday, I watched Trey who is, I admit, unpredictable at best. He should have communicated the fact that Josh is vulnerable and you must continue to do as I say."

"I already understood that."

Horton lifted his arms in an exaggerated gesture of sympathy and Kir loathed him a little more. "*I* thought so."

Kir felt a tic under his right eye. Horton noticed and reached out to touch the skin. Involuntarily, Kir flinched, while Horton looked disgusted.

"I don't know how Snow could have fucked you all the time. I don't even like to think about it." But he liked to mention it. Because it rattled Kir and the less clearly Kir could think, the better he obeyed.

"Do you understand what you have to tell Sam?"

Kir nodded.

"Say it again," demanded Horton as if Kir were stupid. It was only two sentences. Horrible sentences, but only two.

Kir swallowed. "Josh is dead. A Minder killed him."

"Don't mumble."

Kir cleared his thick throat. "Josh is dead. A Minder killed him."

"Exactly."

*Tell.* Kir clung to that word.

He barely paid attention on the way over though Horton appeared more tense than usual. This meeting carried more weight than those that had gone before, because Josh's brother was not easily cowed or bribed or influenced. At least not when the life of his brother was at stake.

As if Kir would proclaim to the world that Josh was dead. It would bury Josh alive. Did Horton think Kir didn't understand the risk to Josh? To force Sam to believe his brother had died was unthinkable. Kir cast Horton a sideways glance just before they left the limo.

Up the fourteen floors they went. Ushered into an office. With his lightheaded fear, Kir found it hard to breathe. He caught Horton eyeing him with worry. *Careful.* For Horton to abort the meeting at the last minute would be disastrous. Kir tried to ground himself by remembering Josh, his bravery and his strength. It didn't banish his fear but it got Kir to the meeting room. Where Horton insisted Kir appreciate the fantastic view of the city.

Kir and Horton waited for Sam Mackay, not the other way around. So Sam thought a lot of himself. Maybe most brats did, Kir wouldn't know. He'd always been desperate to please and very little else.

With Josh, he'd forgotten how empty he really was. He felt empty again.

"Carl," snapped Horton. It took Kir a moment to realize Horton had used his cover name, and another moment to realize they had company. A stranger had entered the room and Kir's gaze fell upon a tall man of Josh's height and build. Their faces weren't at all similar. Sam was darker than Josh, and his eyes were blue, not gray.

Puzzled by Kir's presence or perhaps by his expression, Sam frowned and asked, "And you are?"

Horton rose. "This is my assistant, Carl Brown. I'm—"

"Mr. Horton," Sam interrupted. They shook hands before Sam turned to Kir to do the same. Sam frowned when Kir's hand trembled in his. "I had thought this a one-on-one meeting." Unlike the other men Kir had recently been instructed to work on, Sam did not appear impressed by Horton.

"Carl, sit down." Horton pointed to a chair, obviously irritated by Kir's demeanor. Kir refused to sit, while Horton muttered something about the importance of Kir's presence.

Sam looked well-dressed, Kir had to admit. What he wore was money. Kir hoped that meant power, because Josh needed someone on his side with power.

Horton turned to Kir expectantly, waiting for his all-important words to act on Sam.

But Kir didn't want to work on Sam so he spoke without force. "I have something interesting to tell you about Josh."

Sam's brows rose. "Oh?"

Horton glanced at Kir, then back at Sam, no doubt looking for the telltale confusion that should have marked this brief manipulation.

None showed on Sam's face. Kir's time was running out.

"About my brother?" prompted Sam.

Horton, though wary, adopted a sympathetic expression that put Sam on alert. He glanced between Kir and Horton and his polished exterior cracked a little. He cared about Josh, thank God.

"Mr. Horton," began Kir and Horton nodded encouragement. "Is holding Josh prisoner while blackmailing—"

Horton reached for his gun.

"Don't move!" shouted Kir. Horton froze, shaking in anger and confusion, quivering with his hand stuck on his holstered gun.

"What the fuck is going on?" Sam watched Horton's strange tremors in appalled amazement, then turned to Kir.

"I'm a Minder."

Sam didn't react to the news.

"Lock the door," Kir ordered, pushing a little.

Sam, despite himself, did just that.

"Listen to me. No matter what they say later, you must believe me. Or they will kill Josh. He is being held at the agency, in its core, I believe. You have to get him out, and fast."

Sam sneered at Kir. "What the fuck are you? One of those woo woo guys you hear stories about?"

"Yes. Get someone to search the agency's headquarters and you will find Josh at the center. Get there before they kill him." To Kir's relief, fear showed on Sam's face. "You don't have much time. I counted on you having the resources. Does the name Trey Walters mean anything to you?"

Sam started, the name giving Kir credibility. "Trey's FBI. He's been helping me look for Josh."

*FBI?* "Trey knows *exactly* where Josh is."

Sam went for his cell. Watching Kir the entire time, he called Trey. Turned pale.

Outside, someone tried to open the door. "Mr. Mackay, are you okay?"

"I'm fine," yelled Sam, dialing someone else. "Go away."

"Mr. Mackay, we have reason to believe—"

Then Sam gave instructions Kir didn't understand. Something about FBI and agency headquarters. All the while, the man outside insisted ever louder that he be let in.

"Just fuck right off," bellowed Sam.

"I'm sorry, sir." The man in the hall broke the window.

"Jesus, that's not necessary." Sam turned. "No—"

It was over. Three men rushed the room. Kir stood, expecting a bullet. But perhaps he still had some value, because he was slammed down to the floor by force, face ground into the carpet as they trussed him up and drugged him into oblivion. During the struggle, they dragged Sam from the office, as if arresting him.

Kir had miscalculated. Josh was lost.

# Chapter Seven

Josh strode across the hospital room to reach the bed where Kir lay unconscious, wired up to more than one machine.

"What happened?" he asked Sam who trailed behind him.

"I told you," said Sam patiently. "They almost killed him with the drugs. They were frightened. I couldn't talk them down."

Josh sank his face into the crook of Kir's free arm and he stirred.

"I'm sorry, Josh. He was very brave, standing there to face them." Sam paused, then added, "The doctors thinks he'll come round."

Josh didn't intend to leave the room until Kir did.

Sam dragged a couple of chairs over. "Why don't you sit down? You're exhausted." He placed the chair beside Kir's bed and Josh sat where he could hold Kir's limp hand. He passed a palm over Kir's head. The agency had shorn his curls.

"He has curly hair," Josh told Sam.

Sam nodded.

"They've treated him very badly."

"He's not the only one." Furious to find Josh imprisoned, Sam had already filed Josh didn't know how many suits.

Something about physical abuse because of the fist fight, though that was the least of Josh's concerns.

"Can you protect Kir legally?"

"Oh, I think so," Sam drawled. "It's no longer possible to keep the agency and their 'clients' secret from the general population. The publicity has been Trey's goal all along and with our help he succeeded." Sam sounded bitter because Trey had played Sam, pretending he didn't know where Josh was, when Trey had known everything. "The public knowledge will have consequences. But there is the fundamental issue of human rights." His voice dropped. "It may be necessary to haul out Kir's horrible childhood to discredit the agency and its work."

Josh squeezed Kir's hand tighter.

They sat in silence for a while and Josh tried to think of how to thank his brother.

"You should have contacted me," said Sam, still angry about that. "I would have helped you when you were on the run."

"I didn't want to drag you into this mess and get you killed." Josh had made himself believe his brother didn't care because he couldn't endanger Sam.

"*I* would have asked you for help."

"But you're my baby brother."

Sam shook his head. "Believe it or not, I'm an adult. Kir's age, in fact."

Josh opened his mouth to thank Sam for saving his life and Sam abruptly rose, cutting him off. "You look skeletal these days. I'm getting us food. I'll also have a cot brought in, since you're not leaving him."

"Thank you, Sam."

"Don't thank me."

"Too late."

Sam just punched his shoulder affectionately.

Later, after Sam had gone home for the night, Trey came in to visit. To Josh's dismay.

"How is he?" Trey had betrayed everyone. Except perhaps himself.

Josh didn't know what to make of Trey's concern for Kir. "The doctors think he'll be okay."

Trey walked over to the bed and looked down at Kir.

"Why bring us in, Trey?"

Trey turned his pale eyes on Josh. "I think it was worth it. If you'd stayed at my safe house, I could have kept better control. But you didn't."

"So, you have what you wanted?"

"I'd say so. The agency will be dismantled."

"Good thing for you and your kind."

"Good thing for you," Trey said dryly.

"You can thank Kir for using him when he wakes up."

Trey didn't respond to that suggestion. "He doesn't look much like his sister."

"You've met Maddie?" Josh didn't hide his surprise.

"I helped her escape, long ago." Trey gave a hint of a smile, as if reminiscing.

Josh started. "You didn't join the agency until after Kir escaped."

"I was plain FBI at that point. Not undercover at the agency."

Something inside Josh began to boil. "Why would you allow a seventeen-year-old girl to go free and leave her twelve-year-old brother in that hell?"

Trey's gaze, quiet and assessing, held no guilt or regret. "I didn't know Kir even existed. They were separated by then. I just met a suicidal seventeen-year-old who thought she could manipulate me."

"She doesn't know you helped her?"

Trey shook his head. "I had a soft spot for her. It was all her anger. You'll have to forgive me. I waited till she left Kir's apartment before the agency arrived. I could delay that long."

"You had time to delay, yet you couldn't warn me."

"It wasn't about time. They had you and Kir in their crosshairs, not Maddie." Trey eyed Josh. "You don't look too impressed, given that you're more attached to Kir than his sister. But Kir can adapt. As a teenager, Maddie was breaking."

"Kir breaks, too."

Trey briefly shut his eyes in recognition of the truth in Josh's words. Then he said, "You needn't fear you'll see me again. I plan to disappear."

"Well, I'd better say goodbye then."

Trey nodded and left the room.

Later that night, Josh crawled into bed with Kir and found Trey's words echoing in his head. "You don't break, Kir, okay?" Josh kissed Kir's cheek. He didn't answer, just breathed. At least his sleep seemed peaceful. In time, Josh slept, too.

♋ ♋ ♋

The nightmares had returned. Black hood over head. Mouth taped shut. He would suffocate. Again. This time his hands were free and yet useless, heavy like lead. He needed to lift them, bring them to his mouth and rip off the tape so he could speak.

"Kir."

The voice tried to lull him. Kir struggled to understand where he was. Then strong arms and warm breath surrounded him. Someone said, "It's me, Josh," and Kir, fearing for Josh more than anything, rose fighting.

"Open your eyes, Kir," urged the voice. He tried once, twice, before the heavy lids lifted and he was face-to-face with Josh, who held him tightly, as if Kir might try to get away.

Josh's gray eyes swam with tears. Josh didn't cry.

Kir blinked, confused, wondering if they were dead.

Josh started kissing him, forehead, cheek, mouth, cheek. Tears dropped on Kir's face. Kir's stampeding heart began to subside.

Josh pulled back to look at Kir again.

"Josh?"

"Yup."

"We're alive?" Kir asked.

Josh grinned down at him. "Yes."

Kir looked around and realized he was attached to...something, with tubes and such. "Are we in prison?"

"Nope. We're just waiting for you to get better. They overdosed you." Josh's face clouded at that statement.

"Where's Horton?"

The grin returned, Josh made ridiculously happy by the question and Kir couldn't help returning the smile. "*Horton* is in prison."

Kir blinked, unable to believe it. "No."

"Yup. FBI isn't too happy with him."

"FBI?" Kir felt slow on the uptake but then Josh kissed him and in the moment he didn't care.

"They're closing down the agency."

"Who will hunt us now?" Kir glanced around, trying to assess their situation. His question had Josh wiping his eyes and Kir felt bad, but still confused and exhausted.

"No one *can* hunt us now."

Kir winced. That was a nice dream, but he hadn't the energy to argue. In fact, his eyes drifted shut, though Josh still held him tight. The rest of the night passed in a blur. Some strangers visited—nurses and doctors concerned about his health—and Josh remained by his side.

He woke enough the next day to urge Josh to flee and Josh responded by cradling Kir's face in his hands, his expression fierce "I don't think you understand—we're free and *I am not leaving you.*"

"Josh, I don't know what's going on, but you need to get out of here before people realize what I am."

"No, I don't. You have rights, Kir."

"Rights," he repeated.

"Yes, my brother is going to make sure your rights are recognized."

The brat? "Why would he do that?"

Josh began to look a little exasperated. "Sam knows I love you."

Kir realized he was gaping at Josh's declaration before Josh swooped down to kiss his open mouth. When Josh pulled back, Kir cocked his head. "You love me. You never said that before."

"It's a special occasion. Don't make me repeat it." The glint in Josh's eye gave away his deadpan delivery.

"You're joking."

"I *might* repeat it. You never know. Freedom works in strange ways."

"We're free."

"Kir." Josh appeared pained. "Don't you believe me?"

"I know, I'm repeating myself." He lowered his voice. "But I've never been free, Josh."

Josh's gaze intensified. "You're not entirely free, babe. You're stuck with me."

"That's a good thing, Josh."

"Yeah, it is."

# About the Author

Joely Skye is an introvert, a Spooks (MI5) fan, a wife and a mother. One of her favorite books ever is Ellen Kushner's *Swordspoint* and, while she doesn't watch much TV, she couldn't resist *Queer as Folk*.

She writes male/male romance. Don't ask her why. Men fascinate her, as does romance, so gay romance is the perfect fit.

To learn more about Joely Skye, please visit http://www.joelyskye.com/. Send an email to Joely at mailto:Joely.Skye@gmail.com or join her Yahoo! group to join in the fun with other readers as well as Joely. http://groups.yahoo.com/group/joelyskye/

She also writes as Jorrie Spencer (www.jorriespencer.com).

# Look for these titles

*Coming Soon:*

Marked

# FLY AWAY

## Discover the Talons Series

5 STEAMY NEW PARANORMAL ROMANCES
TO HOOK YOU IN

Kiss Me Deadly, by Shannon Stacey
King of Prey, by Mandy M. Roth
Firebird, by Jaycee Clark
Caged Desire, by Sydney Somers
Seize the Hunter, by Michelle M. Pillow

AVAILABLE IN EBOOK—COMING SOON IN PRINT!

# GET IT NOW

## MyBookStoreAndMore.com
GREAT EBOOKS, GREAT DEALS . . . AND MORE!

Don't wait to run to the bookstore down the street, or waste time shopping online at one of the "big boys." Now, all your favorite Samhain authors are all in one place—at MyBookStoreAndMore.com. Stop by today and discover great deals on Samhain—and a whole lot more!

LaVergne, TN USA
05 August 2010
192250LV00003B/38/A